MORE TALES
OF THE WEST RIDING

MORE TALES
OF THE WEST RIDING

by

PHYLLIS BENTLEY

LONDON
VICTOR GOLLANCZ LTD
1974

© Phyllis Bentley 1974

ISBN 0 575 01898 4

The Secret © 1968 Davis Publications Inc. First published in
ELLERY QUEEN'S MYSTERY MAGAZINE

MADE AND PRINTED IN GREAT BRITAIN BY
THE GARDEN CITY PRESS LIMITED
LETCHWORTH, HERTFORDSHIRE
SG6 1JS

CONTENTS

I

Past Events

THE SECRET (1890)

CRUEL AS THE GRAVE (1880)

LEILA (1900)

OUT TO TEA (1903)

WATER, WATER (1910)

"ONE OF OUR HEROES" (1848–1974)

THE SECRET*

1890

S I M O N A N D H A R R Y Emmett, cousins, both thought
well of themselves. Both, also, having lost their parents in a
typhoid outbreak, lived in Marthwaite with an old mutual
aunt; both, in the early 1890's, worked in the pressing-shop
at Syke Mill; both took the crowded first tram of the day and
swayed in rhythm with its bumpy passage down the West
Riding Ire Valley to their place of employment. Both were
powerful men with the sinewy arms needed for the heavy job
they did together, which in those days consisted of folding
many yards of cloth backwards and forwards over sheets of
heavy brown cardboard "press papers" by hand, then carrying the massive piles thus composed across to one of the six
tall presses, and screwing it down by hand. Both when going
to work wore the clogs, the cloth caps, the wool mufflers, then
customary for men in their position. Both Harry and Simon
were fair in hair and complexion.

But in all other respects they were entirely different, almost
opposite, you might say. They even liked themselves for
entirely different reasons.

For Harry was tall, robust in frame and good-looking in a
rather florid sort of way. His eyes were blue, his cheek fair,
his lips moist and red, his hair thick and curly; he was cheerful and laughed a good deal, perhaps rather more than a

* © 1968 Davis Publications, Inc. First published in Ellery
Queen's Mystery Magazine.

sensible man should. He drank a bit and would have drunk more but that he wished to maintain his local reputation as a successful wrestler; he was a great one for girls, who adored him. In all these matters Harry took a light-hearted pride, and for all these matters Simon despised him.

For Simon was short and, though muscular and tough, hardly seemed to have enough flesh to cover his bones— "scraggy", Harry cheerfully called him. His fair hair, though it attempted a mild wave, was thin and always appeared as if plastered to his skull; his eyes were grey and chilly. His head, however, was large and nobly shaped; and he was conscious that its contents were much superior to Harry's. He enjoyed a drink, but took one rarely; he had not yet seen a girl he fancied and was not going to embark on sex relations till he did. He was honest, conscientious, altogether reliable if not very sunny. His employers approved him, the more serious of his workmates liked him well enough.

One morning on his way to work—it was January, and the Ire Valley was still shrouded in wintry dusk—Simon from his seat in the tram observed Harry, who was standing, strap-holding, in lively talk with a man and a couple of girls who stood around him. Simon knew the man; he was a pleasant good-natured fellow named William Brearley, gamekeeper to one of the groups of manufacturers—the owner of Syke Mill was in another such group—who leased part of the wild moorland above Marthwaite for shooting purposes. Brearley, though only in his twenties like the Emmetts, was already provided with a comfortable cottage up in a fold of the hills, and from the way he held the arm of one of the girls to steady her and coloured pleasantly at Harry's jokes on the subject, it seemed likely he was contemplating matrimony with her.

Simon gave the girl (Alice Shepherd, he remembered, by name) a shrewd look, and approved. A nice, good, ordinary girl, he decided; brown eyes, brown hair, pointed chin; joking back at Harry staunchly without saying anything beyond modesty; nice enough but not very interesting. He would need more than that for himself. His glance moved away.

Ah! This, it appeared, was Alice's younger sister, Emily. Very like Alice, too, but all the world away. Those large, dark, loving eyes in the heart-shaped face, that cloud of dark hair beneath her shawl, the lovely rose of her cheek, her delicious, rather pale lips curved in a gentle smile, the air of sweet timidity, of shy refinement. Her shawl slipped from head and shoulders as she looked up; her bosom, he saw, was soft and full.

Something stirred in Simon's heart. Alice and William were, he gathered, to marry at Easter. Harry Emmett was to be William's best man. As Harry's cousin, Simon could surely contrive to be invited to the wedding feast. From then on, he would press steadily to his goal. He was earning well, he could afford to marry.

In the next few months Simon daydreamed often about his Emily. Quite often he saw her in the morning or evening tram, for Alice and Emily were "menders" at Syke Mill; he observed her keenly, and was ever more satisfied. They grew to nodding acquaintance; the bend of her head was shy and graceful. They spoke; the words they exchanged were only those of greeting and farewell, but they were enough to reveal her voice as sweet and low. Simon imagined himself at Alice's wedding in Marthwaite Baptist chapel, at the party afterwards in the Sunday School. He would sit next to Emily and begin his courtship.

Towards the end of these three months Harry developed a habit of travelling on the upper deck of the tram, always occupied by men only, because there one was allowed to smoke. Thus he came into no contact with the Shepherd girls. It seemed to Simon, too, that Harry's greetings to Alice and Emily as they left the tram had also become curt or non-existent. Was it possible, perhaps, that Harry had divined his cousin's attachment and wished to keep out of the way? Nothing less likely from the careless Harry! Still, it was an agreeable thought.

Then, one morning in early spring, it chanced that the upper deck was full before the cousins reached it and Harry, Simon and the two girls were grouped as on the morning when Simon first noticed Emily. (Simon usually secured a seat for himself, for he was prompt and claimed his rights.) Emily looked up at Harry. Her look was timid, beseeching, not quite venturing to be reproachful, but deeply sad. Harry looked back at her with a friendly, not ill-pleased but teasing smirk. At once Simon knew the whole story.

As the cousins passed through the great mill gates together, Simon grasped Harry's arm and muttered brutally in his ear:

"You've got that girl into trouble."

"Which girl?" said Harry, laughing.

"Emily Shepherd."

"Well, where's the harm?" said Harry cheerfully. "We can be wed. There's plenty of time yet."

But in this Harry was wrong, for by eleven o'clock that morning he was dead. As Harry and Simon were carrying a piece of cloth interspersed with press papers to the press, Harry's foot slipped forward, he fell on his back, his grip was jerked loose, and the whole massive load (more than a hundredweight) came down on his belly. Simon stood transfixed, pale and breathless, clutching the other side of the pile till his muscles gave way and he was obliged to lower it to the ground. The foreman cried in anguish:

"He's nowt but a bloody mess!"

It was too true.

At the inquest the verdict was, of course, *accidental death*. The foreman's repeated bewilderment that a skilled worker like Harry Emmett—a wrestler, nimble on his feet, too— should slip at a job he'd done for upwards of three years was partly assuaged by the discovery of a patch of oil on the sole

of Harry's right clog—he must have stepped into some oil
on his way across the mill yard beside the engine room. The
coroner made some rather cutting remarks about keeping
working premises clean, and Mr Brigg Oldroyd the younger
—old Brigg was getting a bit past work now and left most
of the management details of Syke Mill to his son—was
furious. He paid quite a nice sum in compensation, however,
which of course went to Harry's aunt.

On the night after the funeral, which was well attended,
Simon went to the Shepherds' terrace house. Mr Shepherd,
a very strict Baptist, was out at a Chapel function, as Simon
happened to know, and most fortunately he had taken his
wife with him. It was therefore Alice who opened the door.
She gave Simon a hard look.

"I wanted just to have a word with Emily," said Simon
mildly.

"Well, you can't," snapped Alice, and made to close the
door.

"I'm Harry's cousin, after all," said Simon as before.

An angry exclamation exploded from Alice's lips. "Much
good that'll do us!"

"You might be wrong there," said Simon. His words were
meek but his tone now hard.

Looks of rejection, hope, doubt and perplexity chased each
other across Alice's pleasant face.

"Well, come in then," she said at last, drawing back the
door. "But don't stay long. She's upset, like."

Simon took off his cap and entered. Emily was sitting
huddled by the fire, weeping. The eyes she lifted to him were
full of grief and despair.

"Harry's death has been a great blow to you, lass," said
Simon tenderly.

Tears rolled down Emily's cheeks and she sadly bowed
her head.

"Don't go to upset her now," commanded Alice.

"You clear out and leave us alone," said Simon with sudden ferocity.

"Well," said Alice, taken aback. "I don't know. Well, I'll go upstairs for a minute if you like. Do you want to talk to Simon Emmett, Em, eh?"

"I don't mind," said Emily, completely listless.

"You've only to call if you want me," said Alice, loth to leave her.

Simon gave her an impatient scowl and she hurried off up the narrow stairs.

"Now, Emily," said Simon, drawing up a chair and sitting down beside her: "Stop blubbering and listen to what I say. Your Alice and William Brearley are getting wed come Easter. Lets us be wed on t'same day, eh?"

Emily's eyes opened wide and she stared at him in a kind of horror.

"I can't, Simon," she said faintly at length.

"Yes, you can. I know how it was—" He meant to say *how it was between you and Harry*, but he absolutely could not force out the words, and fell silent. There was a pause. "Child would have his father's name, choose how," he said at length, very low.

"Oh, Simon," murmured Emily, still staring.

"Nobody need ever know. Alice doesn't know, does she?"

"She knows I fancied Harry."

"But about the baby?"

"Not for certain," breathed Emily.

"Well, there you are, then. Your father need never know," said Simon grimly, pressing his point.

As he had expected, a look of fear crossed Emily's face— he knew well enough what her pious father would say when he discovered her moral lapse.

"Say yes. Everyone will be pleased."

"And you, Simon? What about you? Would you be pleased?"

"I've always wanted you, Emily," said Simon.

His absolute sincerity carried conviction.

"You're a good man, Simon," said Emily.

"I shall always be good to you, love. You can count on that."

"And to the child?" panted Emily.

"And to your child. You agree, then?"

There was a pause. Then Emily raised glowing eyes.

"I agree."

"Give us your hand on it," said Simon, smiling.

Her warm, pulsating hand quivered in his which she found cool and sinewy. But it was not only her own reputation, her own future which she thought of as she entrusted herself to Simon; it was the coming child's. He would be safe and cared-for, no bastard, but the legitimate son of a strong and prosperous father. For herself, she would never love any man now Harry was gone; Simon would be as good a husband as any.

They arranged to be married at Eastertide. The Marthwaite folk, when they heard of the approaching nuptials, imagined they had been mistaken when they thought Emily was sweet on Harry Emmett and Harry on Emily.

"Happen it was a kind of cover, like, for Simon."

"Aye. Or happen Harry backed out, like, when he saw Simon was serious."

"Aye, happen. It's true Harry had a dozen girls, he didn't need to take Simon's."

"You'd think a girl would fancy Harry, though, of the pair."

"There's no accounting for women's fancies."

"There is not. Still, Simon's a right decent chap. Steady and that."

"He is. He's all right, is Simon."

Old Mr Shepherd, when he discovered his daughter's condition, gave Simon, to whom he naturally attributed it, a furious harangue about his immoral anticipation of wedlock. Simon listened in silence.

"Don't you care at all for your sin?" thundered Emily's father.

"I regret the matter with my whole heart and soul," said Simon emphatically.

Old Shepherd was somewhat mollified.

At any rate, the secret of Harry's paternity was firmly kept, and Simon and Emily were married at Easter without more than the mild scandal usual in such cases of belated weddings.

They took up their abode with the old aunt. She, however, had been broken in spirit by Harry's death, for he had always been her favourite, and physical decay, accompanied by the customary lack of control of foot and hand, soon followed mental incoherence. Emily tended her with loving care, but it was not long before Simon was summoned from work by the news that his aunt had had a serious fall. She died two days later. The landlord of the cottage was perfectly willing to rent it to Simon, but though at first Simon seemed to mean to accept this offer, his intention presently wavered. This was after his wife had been delivered of a son, a fair, pretty, delicate child who was baptised as Wilfred.

When Wilfred was a month or two old, Simon asked for an interview with the owner of Syke Mill. He was shown into the presence of Mr Brigg Oldroyd the younger, who turned on him one of those piercing glances which his workmen had learned to dread. His tone, however, was not unkind as he asked Emmett his errand.

"William Brearley, my brother-in-law, tells me your lot are wanting a gamekeeper for your shooting on Marthwaite Moor."

"That is so."

"I should like to apply for the job."

• •

"But why?" said Brigg, surprised. "You know nothing about gamekeeping."

"Aye, but I do. I've been about with William Brearley a lot, and he's taught me the job."

"You've a good job here. You're a good worker, and I've been expecting to promote you to foreman in a few years."

"I want to leave."

"Why?"

"That's nobody's business but mine," muttered Simon.

"That is true," said Brigg coldly. As he spoke he remembered having heard something, some sort of gossip, about Emmett's wife. He added in a more sympathetic tone :

"Are your workmates making you uncomfortable?"

"They'd best not try," said Simon grimly.

There was a pause. Brigg observed that sweat stood on the man's forehead.

"Well, I can't promise anything, but I've reason to believe you're an honest man and a conscientious worker, so I'll recommend you to our shooting syndicate. But I think you're making a mistake, Emmett, to leave a good job for some foolish notion."

"I can't seem to fancy the place since Harry—died," blurted Simon.

"Ah. I see. I respect your feeling. I'll recommend you," said Brigg, nodding dismissal.

Simon obtained the gamekeeper's post, and he moved with Emily and his cousin's child to a neat stone cottage in a fold of the moors, built for their gamekeeper by the shooting syndicate. It was a remote spot, though with a handy stream and a glorious view. Simon was happy there. Something in the bleak landscape—the dark rocks, the rough pale grass, the purple heather, the stubborn winds raging over the long slopes—fed his soul, and he enjoyed "keeping down" the vermin. Besides, it was good to be alone, not always on one's guard. Nobody asked what Emily thought about the move,

17

and Emily offered no comment. She had always been quiet and submissive, and she continued in this dutiful trend. Emmett was a considerate and devoted husband and in good employment, and they lived in modest but dependable comfort. Pity they had no (or, no more) children.

In fact the Emmetts enjoyed a quiet peace for several years, until little Wilfred began to walk and talk and play. It then appeared that unfortunately he was a little—it is difficult to find a word, for the disability was very slight, but he was really a little silly, a little "wanting". His eyes were very wide and bright, his laugh shrill and loud; he ran about grinning, he asked silly questions and pestered people, and if rebuked burst into violent tears. When he had a bad cold, which was all too often, he kept his mother on the run all day, wanting this and that, calling her to his bedside and clinging frantically to her when she came.

"It's strange a sharp 'un like Simon Emmett should have such a daft lad," mused Marthwaite men.

"Well, you never know with children," replied their wives. "Besides, Emily—she's not over clever."

"True. Happen that's what's wrong."

"And she spoils Wilf."

"She does. But Simon's a good father. He does his best, choose how."

But as Wilfred grew into a thin, lanky, febrile boy and his overbright eyes, his high giggle, his long clumsy feet, his sudden frenzies, remained permanent features of his personality, Marthwaite's respect and sympathy for Simon in his handling of the boy turned to a certain irritation. The truth was, Wilfred's silliness increased and became tiresome. At times Marthwaite actually expressed its irritation to Simon, who received it in dour silence.

"I'm sorry Wilf's been a bit trying tonight, William," said Simon to the Brearleys as they left the Emmett's cottage one Sunday after an evening of silly, maddening exhibitionism on Wilfred's part. The boy had upset his teacup, reached across the table to snatch a scone, at his mother's mild rebuke pulled a face and struck out at her, struggled wildly, wailing, when Simon gently but firmly restrained his hands, and later continually interrupted the grown-ups' talk round the fire by childish demands for attention.

"I don't know how you can put up with it, Simon," said Brearley, his usually kind tones rough with vexation. "I couldn't be so patient with him myself. If I were your father I'd give you a good clout over the ear-hole," he said sharply to Wilfred, who was dancing, giggling, round the departing guests. "It might do him good, you know, Simon."

"I don't like to upset Emily," said Simon lightly, glancing back at his wife. "She dotes on him, you see."

"Emily spoils him," said Alice with some asperity.

If they only knew, thought Simon, compressing his lips, what an iron control he had to exercise over himself to behave calmly over Wilfred's silly escapades, so foreign to his own decorous inclinations! But of course Emily had suffered a shock from Harry's death, while she was carrying the boy; hence his disability; there was no more to be said.

Wilfred reached the age of twelve, and a new trouble arose.

"He wants to go and be a half-timer, Simon," said Emily.

"Oh, nonsense," said Simon. "Why should he want to go into the mill so young?"

"Two of Alice's boys go. They're his cousins, after all."

"William and Alice have four children to rear, we've one. I can well afford to keep him full time at school."

"Your father doesn't want thee to be a half-timer, Wilf," said Emily gently to her son when he returned from school.

Wilfred threw himself on her breast with a wailing cry.

"I want to go. I want to go wi' Bill and Jack."

Emily's arms closed about him and she rocked him gently to and fro with that glowing look of love in her soft dark eyes which always turned Simon's bowels to water. "Never mind, love. Never mind."

"I want to go," wailed Wilfred.

"You're too young yet. We want you at home for a while yet," said Simon.

Throbbing with fury—for the matter was one of status—and with frustration because he had no child of his own, Simon yet commanded his tone to a decent mildness as he told this lie.

Wilfred looked up from his mother's breast and cried shrewdly:

"No, you don't. I want to go wi' Bill and Jack," he repeated, sticking out his heavy lower lip.

"After all, Simon, if he doesn't go to the mill, where will he go?" said Emily. "When he gets a bit older, I mean. I mean—on the moors with you—I don't think—"

Her voice trailed away, submissive as always, but in this case she spoke sense, reflected Simon. Wilfred could certainly not be trusted with a gun.

The argument—mute on Emily's part, hysterical on Wilfred's, outwardly calm on Simon's—continued for several days. Eventually Simon, as he had expected from the first, gave in. Application had to be made to the head teacher at Marthwaite school, regulations explained, exemption from school sought. It appeared that Wilfred would be obliged to put in some three hundred attendances at school every year. This sounded a large number, but when worked out meant only a few hours at school, morning or afternoon, each week. The rest of his time he could spend at a mill.

"I can't see how they learn anything," grumbled Simon.

"He wants to go, Simon," said Emily softly.

"That's you all over, Emily, you give in to what anybody wants," thought Simon, remembering (of course) her surrender to Harry's wishes.

But he did not say it aloud. Instead, though it was September, the height of the shooting season, he made time to go doggedly down the Ire Valley to Syke Mill to ask for a half-timer's job for Wilfred.

"You, Emmett? I hope you're not wanting to change your job again?" said Brigg.

"No. I hope I give satisfaction on t'moor," said Simon.

"You do."

Simon made his request. Brigg raised his eyebrows and thus confirmed Simon's private view : that Wilfred was dragging him down, would always drag him down. The request, however, was granted. Simon went off up the moor having made, he thought, all necessary arrangements for the boy's début as a half-timer next Monday, but sore at heart.

It was afternoon by the time he got home. Emily was pleased when he told her of his arrangements for Wilfred, and this further darkened his mood. Having snatched a hasty meal, he took down his gun from above the hearth and went out to empty and reset his traps. Stoats, weasels, foxes and poachers were his eternal enemies—nothing scared off poachers more than the sight of a gamekeeper with a gun, reflected Simon grimly. The weekend would see a big shoot on his moor, and he meant his employers to have plenty of birds available.

Suddenly, towards the end of the afternoon, Wilfred came running over the edge of the moorland towards him. The boy plunged down into the hollow where Simon happened to be standing, waving his arms and shouting wildly :

"*You* did it! *You* did it!"

"Is there summat wrong wi' your mother?" cried Simon, alarmed.

"No. *You* did it! You didn't want me to go to the mill!"

"What are you talking about, Wilfred?" said Simon in his artificially mild tone, biting back his vexation, for malice blazed in the boy's mad blue eyes and his thin pale face was horridly distorted.

"*You* told them! *You* made them!"

"Tell me what is wrong, Wilfred," said Simon soothingly.

"The head teacher says I can't have exemption and be a half-timer," panted Wilfred.

"But why not? He told me he thought you could."

"Yes, yes. But now he says he's enquired about me, and I haven't reached the necessary standard of proficiency," screamed Wilfred, blurring and muddling these obviously quoted words. "I can't read."

"What, at twelve years old?" cried Simon.

"Mother's been trying to teach me," whimpered Wilfred. "They haven't time to bother with me, at school. But you told them."

Suddenly all the frightful exasperations of his life—Harry, Wilfred, Emily's love for Wilfred, no children of his own, his own everlasting repression, this imbecile boy impossible to get rid of, his unnecessary humiliation, now doubled, about half-timing, Emily's love for Harry's son—all this boiled up agonisingly in Simon's brain. The fury of years seethed, exploded. He raised his gun, placed it against Wilfred's breast, and fired.

After the shot, a strange silence.

Simon lowered his gun to the ground, leaned on it and sighed heavily.

The boy was dead, it seemed. Yes, he was dead; his body lay sprawled and motionless. Another matter about which Simon must learn to keep silence, for Emily must never know her husband's part in Wilfred's death. Never. The boy's death would break her heart, in any case. For the time. But she would get over it. Wilfred had snatched Simon's gun, of course—it was just the silly sort of thing he would do —and accidentally jerked the trigger and shot himself. Such accidents were always happening. Well! So it was, then. No more Wilfred. A relief, after all!

Simon accepted grimly the task of concealment which lay

before him, shouldered it, sighed and raised his eyes, wondering whether to drag Wilfred home alone, or seek Brearley's help.

On the rim of the hollow stood Brearley, gazing down at him.

"William! Thank God you're here! The boy's shot himself by accident! Help me take him home!"

"I saw you," gasped Brearley, his eyes starting, his throat choked, with horror. "You shot him. I saw you."

"No!" cried Simon, springing forward.

Brearley turned and fled.

Simon, fiercely clutching his gun, chased him headlong over the wiry heather, the tussocks of rough grass, the black peaty marsh. For a moment he disappeared from view, but when Simon bounded up a slope, Brearley lay crouched face downwards in the hollow beyond—he had tripped, perhaps, or perhaps merely sought to hide from his pursuer. Simon sprang down and shot him dead, the bullet entering behind his ear.

Again the strange silence, into which presently intruded the sound of the rising wind and his own gasping breath.

After a while, these calmed, and Simon became capable of rational thought. Well! His story must be changed now. Some poacher must obviously have been come upon by Brearley, and shot him when threatened with arrest— Brearley had no gun with him. The boy Wilfred had by chance seen the murder and fled, been caught and killed by the murderer in fear for his life. But Simon could not know of this, must not know of this; best to go home and act complete ignorance; concern at Wilfred's continued absence could arise later, leave it to Alice to worry when her husband did not return. Pity about Brearley. Always a pleasant chap. Simon cleaned his gun and returned home.

"Wilfred not home yet?" he said to his wife.

"He came, but he went out on t'moor to seek you."

"Oh? He didn't find me."

"He were worried, like, because teacher said after all he couldn't have exemption to be a half-timer."

"Oh? Why were that?"

"Nay, I couldn't right make it out," said Emily.

This might be true, but it might more probably be an attempt to conceal and diminish the reading trouble. It was Emily's habit thus to try to hide Wilfred's defects and peccadilloes from her husband. Simon knew this habit all too well; it maddened him. But now that Wilfred would no longer cause this trouble, he forgave Emily, smiled lovingly at her and said no more.

As the evening wore on and darkness fell, Emily became very uneasy about her son. She went to the door and stood gazing out into the dark, calling "Wilfred! Wilf!" in her soft tones. The pathos of this appeal which could never be answered, and the look of her perplexed eyes, usually so clear, struck Simon to the heart as he went to console her.

"Sit down, love. He'll come in when he's hungry."

"But where can he be? You didn't see him, did you?"

"I told you, no."

"Happen he's afraid to come now because he thinks you'll scold him for being late."

"Happen he is," said Simon gravely, nodding.

After some repetitions of this scene Simon sighed and took down his jacket.

"I'll go out and have a look for him," he said kindly.

"Thank you, thank you," said Emily, softly wailing. "You're a good father to him, Simon."

To search these miles of rolling moorland was a difficult task at any time, in the dark almost impossible. Though Simon knew the moors well, nobody would be surprised by his lack of success in a night search. He tramped about, however, to give an air of verisimilitude to his proceedings, and as the night turned wet and wild, rain on his shoulders and peaty mud on his boots lent support to the tale he would have to tell. It occurred to him to conceal Wilfred's body, though not too deeply; a delay in its discovery, he thought, a little mystery, would be useful in clouding the true course of events. Dragging the body behind a rock, he covered it with earth and bracken. Brearley's body, since it lay on the stretch of moor in Brearley's care, he thought it safe to leave exposed.

He returned home to find Brearley's two sons in his kitchen, making anxious enquiries about their father. Had Uncle Simon seen him?

"No. But I shouldn't worry yet. He'll be out after poachers," said Simon. "Tell you what," he added as the boys' faces remained troubled: "If he isn't back by morning, I'll go down to Marthwaite and tell the police. He might have met up with Wilfred—one of them might have had an accident, and the other not like to leave him, you know. Aye, we'll get the police to search."

This plan was carried out next morning, neither of the missing persons having returned. Not only police, but unofficial Marthwaite men, in instinctive goodwill, took part in the search. These latter turned first to Brearley's beat, for they thought his disappearance more serious than that of an irresponsible boy, who might merely have run away and be in hiding. They soon found the dead gamekeeper, and observed that he was not carrying a gun. The police, to Simon's (concealed) chagrin, found Wilfred sooner than he had hoped, for one of them perceived the metal tips of Wilfred's clogs glittering in the sunlight to which the stormy night had given place, and the body was unearthed.

"Fancy leaving his feet uncovered!" said a young policeman. "Seems daft to me."

"Murderer didn't know he'd left feet uncovered. Lad was buried in the dark, that's what it means," deduced the sergeant.

"Aye, it would seem so," agreed Simon with a puzzled look.

"How do you see it, then, Mr Emmett?" asked the sergeant.

"Brearley caught a poacher, and the poacher shot him, and Wilfred saw it, and the poacher chased him and shot him to prevent him telling, that's how it looks to me."

"What, a poacher in daylight?"

"Nay, it might have been in t'dark. Or twilight falling dark."

"That's so."

When Wilfred's lifeless corpse was carried across the threshold of his home, Emily gave a great cry and fell unconscious, clutching at her son's cold hands as she fell. She lay in bed for several days, hardly moving. Simon, seeing her so distraught, understood better the magnitude of her collapse after Harry's demise. He gave her tender and unceasing care.

Meanwhile, the account of the course of events which Simon had devised to cover the two deaths was generally accepted, and the thought of an imaginary poacher filled men's minds. An entirely innocent man who had—it came out at the inquest and he admitted it frankly—been shooting that afternoon on the free, unleased portion of the moor, was suspected, questioned, arrested, brought before the Annotsfield magistrates, remanded in custody. When this suspicion was first voiced to Simon he was staggered. But he instantly commanded himself.

"I hope he gets off," he thought, "but I can't tell the truth, choose how. It would kill Emily. Nay, I know nowt of it," he said aloud in a worried tone. "I just don't know. I heard shots on the moor that afternoon, that's true."

By the time resumed hearing before the magistrates took place, Emily was well enough to attend, and insisted upon doing so.

Some Annotsfield men who did not know Simon's reputation as an honest man and a good father had been giving him rather odd looks lately when he went to the town on errands, so as Simon set out for the magistrates' court he felt quite uncertain as to whether he would return thence as an accused murderer or no. Accordingly he dressed himself very neatly, and shaved with special care. As he climbed the steps to the court, with Emily and Alice in deep mourning beside him, he felt himself the mark of every eye, and carried himself with stony dignity. In spite of his short stature and thinning hair, his appearance commanded respect; the lofty carriage of his large head showed him as a man not lightly to be distrusted. The innocent accused, pale and hangdog, looked far more guilty than he, reflected Simon with satisfaction.

This time, however, the accused man had secured from somewhere a sharp shrewd counsel, who produced and proved—not perhaps quite to the hilt but enough to convince any reasonable mind—an alibi for his client. The magistrates recalled Simon to the witness box.

"Hold hard," he urged himself as he calmly rose. "Keep the secret."

He set his jaw, advanced with a firm regular tread and gave his replies in a quiet steady tone.

The magistrate took him again through his own meagre story of the day of the murder, and then, to his surprise, began to ask him questions about Wilfred.

"Was the boy quite normal?"

"He was a little backward," replied Simon.

"How backward?"

"Well—he couldn't read very well."

"At twelve years old?"

"His mother was trying to teach him," said Simon rather hastily, alive to a hint of censure.

"Backward, yes. But was he ever violent?"

"Never," said Simon emphatically. "He was a gentle, eager boy."

"Was he fond of his uncle?"

"His uncle?" repeated Simon, amazed.

"His uncle, William Brearley. Had his uncle not scolded him at times?"

With a shock Simon perceived that they suspected Wilfred of having shot his uncle and then himself, and Simon of having come upon the body and to conceal his son's crime removed the gun and buried Wilfred. This might have been a convenient hypothesis but for its effect upon Emily, who was already flushed and panting under its mere suggestion. He made haste to discredit it.

"Wilfred was always fond of his uncle. He went a good deal to Brearley's place, and played with the two boys, his cousins."

"Had Wilfred ever handled a gun?"

"Never. He was never allowed to touch a gun."

"Did you ever teach him how to fire a gun?"

"Never."

"Could he have had a gun in his possession, even for a few moments, on the afternoon of the murder?"

"Impossible. I had my gun with me, and as you've heard my sister-in-law say, Brearley left home without his gun."

The hearing ended with the discharge of the innocent accused, and without any other accusation being made.

"I'm glad he got off, for I don't think he did it," said Simon soberly as he drove Alice and Emily home in the trap he had hired.

The sisters were too sunk in grief, it seemed, to reply. But when, having left Alice at the cottage she must soon vacate, the Emmetts presently found themselves in their own home, Emily turned her dark luminous eyes steadily on her husband, and asked in a low tone:

"Who do you think killed my son, Simon?"

"We shall never know," replied Simon with a sigh.

He sighed because he felt the burden of secrecy, the need to conceal, heavy upon his shoulders. It would rest there, he knew, till the day he died.

Sometimes in the years that followed, he felt the burden almost intolerable. It was his first thought in the morning, his last at night: keep the secret. *Occasionally* when he was out on the moors in the driving winds and bright cold sunshine of March, the still shimmering heat of August, the white dazzling snow of January, he felt a lifting of the heart, as if he might be about to be happy; but instantly the weight of the secret closed down on him again and forbade it. (The feeling he had when he took the passive Emily in his arms was entirely different: a hot passion, a guilty unrelenting triumph.) Again, when he helped Alice to regain her job as mender, supervised her removal back to Marthwaite—her parents took her in—presently found jobs for her growing sons and "gave away" her daughter in a suitable marriage, Simon smiled to himself and felt a warmth about his heart. But in a moment the warmth chilled and his heavy features hardened again into sternness; he could not afford to relax.

The years rolled on. Simon lived a life of impeccable integrity; prospered in his work; saved money; bought some cottage property in Marthwaite which proved a good investment. He was a devoted and considerate husband, a kind and helpful uncle—pity he had no children—a most capable secretary and treasurer to various Ire Valley good works he undertook.

All this time, Simon kept his secret. For a few weeks after the moor murders, local discussion raged and diverse and extraordinary theories were propounded, some of them uncomfortable to Simon; but as the months passed the matter grew stale, and presently new generations grew up who had scarcely heard of the event. The strain of the secret aged Simon before his time. His shoulders bowed, his thin hair whitened, his mouth set in a hard line. But he remained a respected figure, and steadily kept his secret from his wife.

The day came when Simon had a stroke. It happened when he was out on the moor with an Oldroyd shooting party. Brigg Oldroyd's son Francis was an excellent shot, and followed his own notions with the impetuosity of youth. Simon's advice had previously kept the shooting butts away from the place of Wilfred's death, but young Mr Francis had demanded that butts should be aligned within twenty yards of that fatal hollow. The position he chose was a good one and Simon could not oppose it, he felt, without displaying an undue sensitivity. He superintended the butts' erection with his customary cold efficiency, but when the first shot rang out from them he fell to the ground.

He found himself in bed in his own home, with the doctor just turning away and Alice and Emily seated at his bedside. From the gravity of their expressions and his own sensations (or lack of them) he perceived at once that he was a dying man. He fixed his eyes on Emily with intense yearning.

"I must be alone with Simon, Alice," murmured Emily. "Leave us together."

Alice bowed her head and left the room.

Yes, he was dying, reflected Simon. Pity. Yet, in a way, he was relieved. In a few minutes his life would be over, and he would have succeeded in his great aim : he would have kept his secret to the end. No longer must he maintain his incessant watch and ward. He felt himself slipping towards the dark. Yes, it was a relief, his success. Emily would now never know. The long struggle was over. He moved his lips to make the motion of a kiss. Emily bent over him. But she did not yield him an embrace. Her eyes were hard and burning.

"I know your secret, Simon," she murmured. "I've always known."

Simon gazed at her in awful horror.

"How—how—"

"In the court, when you told the magistrates I was trying to teach Wilfred to read. You couldn't have known that unless you'd seen him that afternoon. We'd kept all that bother about his reading, from you. I told him, when he went out to look for you, he'd better make a clean breast of it."

"Then why—why—"

"Why didn't I tell on you? I owed you silence, Simon, for marrying me and giving Wilfred a name."

"Emily—"

"I shall never tell on you, Simon, never. But I shall never forgive you."

Simon looked at her lovingly, and smiled, and died.

He smiled with joy. He could still think well of himself, since Emily did not know his secret. For it was not, in fact, a patch of oil which had caused Harry to fall, all those long years ago. Simon with a well-placed foot had tripped his cousin.

CRUEL AS THE GRAVE

1880

I T B E C A M E C L E A R to me later, as you will see, that
there was a deep cause of stress, an emotion indestructible,
whether hostile or friendly or both, between the two men,
before this story opens. One of the people who knew it told
me the whole thing at last. But this happened only very
recently. Even then I had to rely chiefly on my long knowledge of those concerned, derived simply from living with
them for many years. From these sources, once given the
major clue, I have devised, deduced, guessed, whichever
you prefer, some of the incidents which so fatally directed the
story's course.

Certainly my knowledge came scarcely at all from anything my mother vouchsafed on the subject to me. In my
experience emotions in the previous generation always strike
the following generation as either incredible or obscene. So
my mother was not likely to embark upon this matter with
her daughter, even if she knew it. But indeed, as you will see,
she did not know it; half a lifetime was devoted to keeping
her in ignorance.

I might have heard the story from my grandmother,
Hannah, if she had known it and if I had known her in her
younger days. But I am sure that more than half a lifetime
had been devoted to concealing it from her. And in any case
I knew her only in her old age; in black silk dress and shawl,
carrying on her thick faded red hair one of those lace caps

decked with ribbon bows which were the correct wear for old ladies at that time—my grandmother was very particular about the cut and elegance of these caps, which were accordingly the bane of my mother's existence, for she had to make them—and also, presently, of mine, for the same reason.

Many grandmothers, I am told, are very confidential with their grandchildren. Mine was not. In fact, she was something of a terror to us. She had all the vehement temper, the fierce determination, the knowledge that she was Right, which belong to all that side of our family, together with the red hair, the blue eyes, the brilliant complexion. My great-uncle Joshua Milner, who was her brother, had them all too—only, of course, stronger because he was a man.

So though anything that had passed between my great-uncle Joshua Milner and my grandfather Thomas Hallam in their early days may or may not have been known to my mother and grandmother, it certainly was not passed on to me. All my mother told me was that my great-uncle Joshua was rich, owned a large mill, was married in second wedlock to a very handsome woman, great-aunt Ada—who though as handsome as a gipsy was unfortunately not quite what in those late Victorian times was called a lady—and that the pair had a beautiful daughter, Kate, who inherited her father's temper and her mother's long rich dark hair and brilliant dark eyes. Great-uncle Joshua adored his daughter; his wealth was made for her. (His first marriage had been disastrous in respect of children; two miscarriages and an early death.)

My grandfather Thomas Hallam, on the contrary, was one of those deceptively mild men who never shout or make scenes, but as life progresses are found to have natures as firm and unyielding as the millstone-grit of their own Pennines. He too had a beautiful daughter—my mother; whom in his turn he adored. For his Lucy, with her glorious

chestnut hair, blue eyes, fair complexion, deliciously small
and well shaped body, nothing was too good.

My grandfather's antecedents were unknown in the West
Riding; he first impinged on the public consciousness, so to
speak, when he suddenly appeared as the "representative"
and presently "acting manager" of Messrs Joshua Milner.
He was regarded then as an up and coming young man with
pleasant manners, but not too soft for his own good, and
when he courted and presently married Joshua's sister, Ada,
who was several years older than himself, the match was
thought very suitable, advantageous to Hallam in the worldly
sense but not so much so as to excite severe comment. He
bought presently a house, Number 3 Hill Road, on the slope
of the hill above Joshua's substantial and always increasing
mill, and lived there apparently happily with a rather fierce
though loyal and handsome wife and his real beauty of a
little daughter, my mother Lucy.

Thomas Hallam was a good salesman. Honest but agreeable, he knew nothing of cloth when he arrived in the West
Riding, people said, but after all Joshua Milner knew everything about cloth, and Hallam soon learned. In top hat,
morning coat and lemon kid gloves, then the customary
attire to do business in London, his Dundreary whiskers well
brushed, his smile pleasant, his word reliable, he often made
customers in the metropolis. All this was common knowledge,
open to all, and that there were sometimes tiffs between the
two men on details of management was no doubt also fairly
well known in Annotsfield—but not much regarded, for in
the West Riding men were apt to speak their minds. There
was a story for instance that once on Hallam's return from
the capital Joshua shouted at him in such fury about the
prices he had accepted that Hallam urged him to conduct
the rest of the interview in Joshua's mansion, which, as was
so often the case in those days, stood just to one side of the
mill.

"No reason for all Annotsfield to hear our prices," said Hallam mildly.

"That's right," agreed Joshua. "You've some sense, Tom," and he led the way across the mill yard, where several men stood grinning, enjoying the scene. But he spoke grudgingly, and when he reached his own dining room in Milne Thorpe where a large round table stood laden with all the eatables for a Yorkshire high tea—ham and jam, scones and buttered toast and cake darkly heavy with fruit—observing that his wife had set an extra cup for his brother-in-law, his anger exploded. Seizing the edge of the table in his strong hands, he raised it with a sharp pull and tilted it. Everything at once slid off the table with a resounding crash.

"What will you do next, you daft fool!" shouted Ada.

Hallam, however, nimbly stepping round the table, retrieved the huge silver teapot as it fell and placed it in safety. It was hot, of course.

"Burned your hands, Tom?" enquired Joshua, laughing.

"Somewhat," returned Hallam in his usual mild tone, drawing out his spotless handkerchief to mop up the liquid which stained his clothes.

This incident—which, as I say, many people in Annotsfield doubtless knew and chuckled over, for the workmen knew it and would of course gossip—might give a hint of an uneasy relationship between the brothers-in-law. But only a hint, for it ended in a hearty snort of laughter from Joshua, a cool smile from Hallam. Only now do I know that such an unease very definitely existed, that from its nature it was indestructible, and that it was exasperated by the unconscious rivalry which materialised between their respective wives about their daughters, Lucy being just over a year younger than Kate.

In their early days, the little girls played together happily. They ran headlong about the mill yard, they chased their highly coloured rubber playing-balls, they skipped, they fell

35

off walls and wept together over the resulting holes in their petticoats which both their mothers strongly deprecated; Mrs Hallam because she mended them, Mrs Milner because she didn't. Sometimes, as little girls will, they acted weddings at which each played a variety of the known parts. On November 5th, and at Christmas time, the girls actually roasted potatoes and chestnuts in the great mill boilers, crying out with excitement and fright when the doors were pushed back and they saw the huge red-hot fires stretching away within. For of course the mill workers doted on the pretty little pair, played with them, joked with them, spoiled them —sometimes; sometimes they resented some sharp word carelessly spoken, some arrogance of command from Kate.

"Like your father, you are," they grumbled.

"Aye! Like as two peas. Temper to match."

But as soon as the children began to go to school differences began to emerge. Kate disliked school and was bored by lessons. Lucy rather liked them. Perhaps Lucy was sharper in mind than Kate? She read earlier than Kate, and spelled better and wrote more neatly. In those days red hair was a joke. The pupils at the little one-teacher school down the road teased Lucy about her blazing mane. Soon it was established that Kate was the beautiful girl, Lucy the clever one. Both children unknowingly resented this division, but each was proud of her own distinction. Red hair was an act of God and nothing could be done about it, but perhaps Lucy's home environment showed more intelligence than the Milners'. Hallam, it appeared, had a good deal of taste, and he did not waste his time in London. He often brought gifts home for his darling little Lucy. A frock, a sealskin cap, a sash, a pair of wooden skates, a book.

Then the really awful thing happened. Hallam actually proposed to send his Lucy away to a boarding-school near York, of which he had heard good reports. (It was reputed to be very elegant in tone, and employed a music master.)

Joshua of course thought this silly, high-flown, not to say la-di-da, but wondered uncomfortably whether he should send Kate. His wife screamed when she heard of this.

"What good would it do Kate, for heaven's sake?" she cried. "Kate will get married without music lessons."

"Aye, she will. You'll rue, Tom," said Joshua in an almost kindly tone. "What will the child grow up like, eh?"

"But why not send Kate as well? At the same time as Lucy? Together, you know, they wouldn't feel so lonely."

"Kate'll never be lonely, with her looks," said Joshua with conviction.

"At least ask her," urged Hallam.

Kate floating past the bay window at the moment accompanied by two personable young men, her father threw up the sash and called to her.

"Kate, would you like to go to this smart school near York, with Lucy?" he shouted.

An expression of strong distaste crossed Kate's beautiful face.

"*School!*" she cried in scornful capitals. "No, thank you!"

"Well, there you are, you see," said Joshua with satisfaction, lowering the window.

Lucy accordingly went to boarding-school alone.

A few weeks after she had left home Joshua, meeting Hallam by chance in the handsome warehouse which Milners had built in Annotsfield, said to him:

"So Lucy's bound to learn music, I hear?"

"And French," added Hallam, not without pride.

"I don't know how you're going to pay for all this out of your salary, Tom," said Joshua.

There was a pause. Perhaps Hallam allowed time for a brotherly offer of an increase? None came. So, with a steady look at his brother-in-law, he said quietly:

"We shall manage."

The Hallams not only managed. At the end of her first

term Lucy had made quite a little progress in the musical art; so—

"Have you heard?" shouted Ada to her husband. "He's bought her a piano!"

"Never!"

"He has. It's only an upright, however; that's what your sister says. You go straight down to Annotsfield and buy us a grand."

"What's a grand? What's an upright?"

"Never mind. They'll tell you at shop, soon enough. I'm not going to see our Kate done down by our own commercial traveller, I can tell you."

The grand was duly installed.

Thus was the rivalry as it were cemented. And now a worse feature of it developed. Hallam often brought ladies' magazines, dress patterns, light fabrics, made-up garments, home; the magazines showed fashion pictures, Lucy met fashion at school; so she often appeared in Annotsfield quite elegantly attired. The bitterness was that after she had worn a well-designed cotton frock, Kate at the next party appeared in the same dress—in silk.

A popular entertainment at that time was the Penny Reading, sponsored and organised by the various Sunday schools of the time to give their young people something harmless but lively to do. Members of both sexes sang, played, recited, took buns and tea. Lucy played on the piano and sang, in her sweet but thin little voice, the sentimental tunes of the time—*I Stood on the Bridge at Midnight* and *I Shot An Arrow into the Air* were particular favourites—while Kate giggled in a front seat. For outwardly, of course, Lucy and Kate were still great friends.

At these Readings Kate was always well attended by young men. She was beautiful, she was well dressed, she was not too serious, she could pick up a joke and snap out a reply which made the speaker feel witty, her father was comfortably rich. So, she was a suitable match for any textile young man. It was at one of these Readings—one-penny admission —that the encounter between the pair took place.

Ben Clough was undoubtedly the matrimonial catch of Annotsfield. His ancestors had been clothiers for some three hundred years, progressing from a single loom in a many-windowed weaver's cottage to the massive mill buildings in the valley, known not only in Annotsfield but all over the world, which produced hundreds of thousands of yards of fine worsted cloth every year, and sold them. Ben had a tough old grandfather who knew everything about textiles, a handsome rakish father (rarely seen in Annotsfield) who was rumoured to be too fond of wine and women, a stiff mother of great propriety. Ben himself was not particularly good-looking; rather stocky and sturdy than tall, he had a solid determined face, pleasant enough if you didn't cross him; not attracted by any of the arts, he was yet generally reputed to be no fool. His temper was nothing like as bad as Joshua's, his impulses on the whole were kindly and certainly not mean if you took him the right way; he didn't talk too much, but what he said was always practical. Kate liked him. She met him at a Reading and then at several Readings and at chapel, and at one or two private parties. Seeing how things were going, and pleased by the prospect of such a desirable son-in-law, Joshua urged his wife to give private parties of her own. The rooms in the Milne Thorpe house were large. The Milners rolled up the carpets, pushed back the furniture in one room, set up a very lavish buffet supper in the other, and invited all Kate's young friends by word of mouth. Lucy, with various others similarly qualified, chiefly elderlies, of course, played for the dancing. (Many, I have been told, could play a waltz or a polka; but Lucy, wonderful to relate, could provide a whole set of lancers.)

One January afternoon, when they were skating together on the frozen Clough mill dam, Kate said lightly to Ben :

"You'll come on Thursday, Ben?"

"Of course."

He paused; Kate with unusual sensitivity perceived that there was more to come. She waited.

"Do something for me, Kitty," said Ben at last. "Will you?"

Kate was delighted to be called Kitty, particularly as Ben used this pet-name only in private. But remembering her mother's warnings, she said, though careful to use a flirtatious note: "Depends what it is."

"Ask Edward Randal to your party."

"Which is Edward?"

Ben pointed out a tall slender boy, dark with waving hair, decidedly handsome, who at this moment chanced to shoot past them, skating admirably and smiling at them as he went.

"He skates well," she said in a neutral tone.

"Aye. He is good at rugger too," said Ben. "And dances fine. He's a friend of mine. In fact," he added with an air of taking the plunge, "he's my best friend. He's apprenticed at our mill."

"Oh, really," said Kate coolly, not in the least interested in a mere apprentice.

Ben however proceeded to narrate Edward's history. His father had died young, leaving his widow and children rather scantily provided for, but with a small fund particularly allocated to pay for his son's apprenticeship to some great textile firm. The two lads, Ben and Edward, were as different in their souls as in their fortunes. Edward kind, gentle, quiet, but full of mild fun, pleasant-tempered, over-generous, honest and honourable and loving towards every thing and person that lived, as well I should know, seeing that he is my father. Why and how these two different natures clung to each other I do not know. Everyone liked Edward, but why should Edward like Ben? But so it was; they were true friends.

And so Edward came with Ben to the Milners' house, and danced. (As Ben said, he was a brilliant dancer.) Lucy, delicious in her well-cut cotton frock, sat at the piano (grand) for most of the evening, dutifully playing dances. For her aunt Ada kept calling out cheerfully to her:

"You'll play this one for us, won't you, love?"

So what else could she do but sit at the piano, playing? All the same her pretty face took on a tinge of melancholy— or rather cross and sulky—air, for Lucy adored dancing. ("And I danced better than Kate," she told her daughter later, seriously. "Kate was too heavy.")

Embarking on the second set of lancers, sadly because with those various figures to get through a set of lancers was a long job, Lucy found herself actually sniffing with vexation. "If I don't take care I shall cry," she told herself angrily, tossing her bright head to shake away the tears.

This action brought into view the figure of a young man, leaning against the piano and gazing down at her from very kind brown eyes.

"Aren't you going to dance at all?" he enquired in a compassionate tone.

"My aunt likes me to play," said Lucy, telling the whole story in her tone without a word.

"But it's not fair to keep you at it all the time. You've hardly danced at all," said Edward. "Don't you like dancing?"

Lucy laughed, and her face cleared. (She was a very pretty girl.)

"Dance with me next time. I'll wait here. You stand up as soon as the lancers end, and we'll move off together. Yes?"

"Yes," said Lucy.

"And," as Lucy years later often told her daughter, "I always liked him best after that."

41

In a word, at that moment Edward and Lucy fell in love, and remained in love for the rest of their lives.

At first the double courtship was highly convenient. On many an evening, Ben and Edward presented themselves together at Milne Thorpe House or Number 3 Hill Road, and somehow the two girls always seemed to be about together somewhere. The two couples thus chaperoned each other, to the satisfaction of their respective parents. They skated, walked, danced, attended concerts and the theatre, picnicked, ate high tea at one or the other's homes, and were happy.

After leaving the girls at the doors of their respective homes, Ben turned off down to the neighbouring valley where that massive Victorian Gothic mansion Clough Lea, the home of the Cloughs, stood, and a comfortable bed awaited him. Edward, on the contrary, walked briskly up the hill to the Clough mill, had a word with the night watchman, who knew him well, entered the warehouse, and throwing himself down on a handy piece of damaged cloth, slept the night there till the morning buzzer, thrilling the air at five-thirty a.m., woke him to the morning's work. He was never late for work, as old Mr Clough had duly noted.

The Hallams smiled, but Joshua did not altogether approve of Edward's courtship.

"He's a very nice lad, Tom," he said seriously. "A very nice lad is your Edward. Quick in the uptake. Kind, and pleasant. And honest. You might say good. Yes, I grant you that. But he hasn't a ha'penny of his own, and he's a mother and two sisters to keep. What he and Lucy are going to live on, I really don't know."

"He knows cloth," said Hallam.

"True, true."

"And Ben Clough is his friend," thought Hallam. He did not say this, but he was not the only man in Annotsfield who

42

saw Edward as the manager of Clough Mills, with Ben as overlord, in the days to come.

Just for a moment, however, Joshua had other views. That night he put them to his wife.

"How do you say if I put that Edward lad into Milners' as manager?" he said.

"Never!"

"Why not? We've no son to carry on, love. He knows cloth. He's going to marry Lucy you know, my sister's child. She's my niece."

"That's why. Don't you see, Kate would always be jealous of him? In her father's business! Lucy's husband? She'd hate it!"

"Jealous?" pondered Joshua. "Why jealous?"

"Kate and Lucy are jealous, surely you know "

"Nay, I haven't seen owt. Why should they be jealous?"

"Well, they are."

"Don't worry, love," said Joshua sardonically. "Yon Edward'll be managing Clough's before you know where you are."

"As to that we shall see."

"It's time young Ben said something to me about Kate," grumbled Joshua, releasing his braces. "If he doesn't come up to scratch soon I shall give him a hint."

"You'll spoil all if you do."

"Well, I'll roll my eyes at him a bit, choose how," said Joshua, laughing.

"You can do that," said Ada cheerfully.

Unfortunately, however—and in the event it proved bitterly unfortunate for all concerned—Joshua, who was not a man for fine shades, rolled his eyes so heavily that Edward perceived it. As the two young men walked off together one summer evening to join the main road Edward said :

"Why was old Milner rolling his eyes at you like that? As if he suspected you of making off with the silver!"

43

His tone was puzzled. But Ben laughed.

"He thinks it's time I said something to him about Kate, I daresay."

"What do you mean?"

"You can't go dangling after a girl for ever without coming out with honourable intentions, or something of the sort. Otherwise it might compromise her."

"Compromise!" exclaimed Edward in horror.

"Well, spoil her other chances, like."

"But it would be the same with Lucy!" cried Edward.

"Of course. Kate has been hinting a bit to me lately, I've thought. Has Lucy said anything?"

"No! No!"

"Well, of course you aren't in a position to marry, yet."

"No. But still—what shall you do, Ben?"

"I'll talk to grandfather. He's quite keen about Kate really. Well, good night."

Edward was left in agony. Compromise! Spoil other chances! People hinting! His darling Lucy!

He dashed to the nearest wall, climbed its low rough-cast hurriedly, knocking off a stone or two, rushed up two hilly fields of rough grass, and pressed the bell of Number 3 hard and long. Thomas Hallam opened quickly.

"Something wrong at the mill?" he cried. Then more calmly: "Oh, it's you, Edward."

"May I have a word with you, Mr Hallam?"

"Of course."

"May I have your permission to pay my addresses to Lucy?"

"Seems to me you've been doing that a long time already, my boy."

"Yes. Well. May we be engaged?"

"You were out of your apprenticeship last New Year's Day, so you're free to get engaged if you want to."

"Yes."

"But you'll have to find a decent income from somewhere before you think of getting married."

"I'll find one!" cried Edward. "I love Lucy, Mr Hallam."

"Oddly enough, I believe you."

"May we be *engaged*, Mr Hallam?" implored Edward with emphasis.

"Well. Yes."

"Thank you, thank you!" cried Edward, seizing his future father-in-law's hands and wringing them so earnestly as to be painful. "May I, could I, see Lucy just for a moment?"

The sound of a sob made Mr Hallam turn. There, in the doorway of the sitting-room, stood Mrs Hallam and Lucy, both weeping.

"Here's Edward come wanting to be engaged to Lucy," said Hallam drily. "I've consented."

Edward and Lucy fell into each other's arms.

Accordingly next morning Lucy, radiant with happiness, ran down the hill to tell her cousin her joyous news.

Kate, naturally, was furious. To be outrun at the post, like this, was more than she could bear. She controlled her rage sufficiently to offer suitable congratulations, a suitable kiss. But her face was still white and her eyes burning when in the afternoon Ben, having had a most agreeable interview re income, house, shares and so on with his grandfather, arrived to formalise his suit. Practical as ever, he tackled Joshua in the mill, then came across to the house smiling, entered the room where his love was waiting for him alone (forewarned), took her hand and exclaimed briskly:

"Marry me, Kate."

"You've been a bit slow in the uptake, my lad," Kate told him. This was risky, but she was too angry to care.

"I *am* slow in the uptake, love," admitted Ben. "But when I get there, I'm there. What have I not done now, eh?"

"There's that hateful little nincompoop, Lucy Hallam, my cousin, got engaged last night. Got engaged before me."

"Well, good for Edward," said Ben laughing. "Edward's my best friend, after all."

"But it's so humiliating for me, Ben; it is really."

"Not a bit," said Ben. "It'll be years before they can get married."

"True. And when were *you* thinking of getting married?"

"How about September?"

"Ben, you are always so sensible," said Kate, smiling.

They kissed, enjoying it a good deal.

Discussions of the most delicious kind about the wedding arrangements now went on between Kate and her mother. Joshua intended the wedding of his daughter to be the biggest and finest ever seen in Annotsfield, and if this cost money he was prepared to spend it. Kate and Ada entirely agreed— that is to say, Ada yielded to all Kate's wishes. On one point, however, Kate was awkward.

"How many bridesmaids do you think, love?" said Ada. "Two, or four?"

"Six!"

"That's going to be costly for Ben, six presents. But I daresay he won't mind. Let's see, there's his cousin Alice, and our Lucy, and—"

"I won't have Lucy."

"What?"

"I will not have Lucy," shouted Kate with a grimace.

"But you'll have to have Lucy, Kate," objected Ada. "She's your father's niece."

"I will not have Lucy."

"But from being children you've always said you'd be each other's bridesmaids."

"I will not have Lucy."

"What are you two shouting at each other about?" said Joshua disagreeably, entering.

"She says she won't have Lucy as one of her bridesmaids," said Ada, timid.

"Yes, you will."

"No, father, I won't. Why should I have my wedding spoilt by Lucy, with her superior airs?"

"Kate, you must have Lucy. Her mother would never forgive me, otherwise."

"Father," said Kate, stretching her face, crimson with rage, stiffly towards him : "I am your daughter and I like my own way as much as you do. I will not have my wedding spoiled by Lucy."

"How could she spoil it?"

"Just by being there. I'll be married in a registrar's office and have no bridesmaids at all, sooner than have Lucy."

"And what will Ben say to that?"

"Ben will do what I wish."

"That remains to be seen, my girl. Ben's a tougher nut than you think."

"Ha !" cried Kate, and laughing and tossing her head scornfully, she ran from the room.

"You'll have to give in to her, Joshua, or the whole thing might break down."

"But what shall I say to Tom?"

"That's your look-out. It's a nuisance, though, for I was hoping Lucy would write out the invitations for us."

"Well, she won't. . . . Tom," said Joshua in a diffident and apologetic tone very different from that of his usual orders, next day: "It seems your daughter and mine have quarrelled."

"Quarrelled?"

"Kate doesn't want to have Lucy as one of her brides-maids."

"What !"

"I'm as vexed about it as you are, Tom, but there it is. She's an obstinate piece, is our Kate."

"She's *your* daughter."

"Aye. That's the way of it."

"In view of everything, you won't expect us to come to the wedding, then," said Hallam quietly.

As he was not a Milner, he did not shout or stamp. But his face was pale, his hands quivered; his tone was like ice.

"But what else could you do, Tom, for heaven's sake?" queried Joshua uneasy.

"We shall go to Blackpool for the day," said Hallam drily.

This insultingly commonplace solution was received with tears of fury in Number 3. Mrs Hallam wanted to rush down to Milne Thorpe and, as she said, "have it out" with her brother. But her husband forbade this, and when Thomas Hallam put down his quiet foot, it stayed down. On this occasion, his daughter approved his decision.

"I don't care a button for Kate's wedding," she said cheerfully—lying, of course. "I don't like the Milners *or* the Cloughs. It's sure to be a thoroughly vulgar affair."

Unfortunately, however, as with a stone thrown into a pond, there were further ripples.

"This is a bad do about Lucy, Edward," said Ben seriously to his friend.

"It's a very bad do. Couldn't you persuade Kate—"

"No. Marrying Kate takes some doing, I can tell you. She's very spirited."

"Like her father."

"Well, yes. Of course when we're married, it'll be different."

Edward doubted this, but did not say so.

"Edward, couldn't you persuade Lucy . . ."

"No! It's an insult to her to suggest it. By the way, Ben," said Edward sadly: "I don't know if you're thinking of me being your best man—"

"Of course I am."

"Well, I can't do it."

"What!"

"I can't do it. Lucy would never get over it." He hesitated and added in a low tone: "I love Lucy, you see."

Ben groaned. "This is awful, awful! Perhaps time will heal it all," he suggested despairingly.

"I doubt it. Lucy's a Milner too, you know. And I may as well tell you now, Ben," went on Edward uncomfortably: "that it's no use my staying on at Clough Mills. Kate would always have her knife into me—and she'll be your wife, you know."

"But what will you do if you leave us, Edward?"

"I've got a chance to go into partnership with a man up the valley," said Edward. "Old Jeremiah Sykes. His son's just died, so he's anxious to get somebody into the firm. Terms are quite good—considering."

"I can't bear it, Edward."

"No, I can't either. But there it is. When you fall in love, you're done for."

"That is so."

"Well—goodbye, Ben."

"Goodbye, lad."

They shook hands and parted.

Ten years later, Lucy was walking down one of the main residential roads into Annotsfield, her two young sons at her side, when she encountered, for the first time since their marriages, her cousin Kate.

It happened in this way. Lucy had been to visit Edward's mother, old Mrs Randal. She was even now rebuking herself for feeling disappointed to find the old lady in good health, recovered from a slight recent influenza. Mrs Randal is a sweet person, Lucy told herself sternly; Edward inherits much of his kind disposition from his mother; of course I don't want her to die. (All the same, it would take some of the burden from Edward's shoulders. No! Perish the thought.) This long highly respectable terrace of middle-class houses was just beginning to be invaded by professional men —a noted surgeon, a fashionable dentist—who enjoyed the solid houses with their long narrow gardens stretching down towards the pavement, terminating in a scrolled ironwork gate and two or three well-built steps.

Lucy's elder son, Edward always called Ned, a tall slim dark-eyed boy very like his father in spirit as well as physique, being mild, firm and courteous, walked sedately at her side. Harry, the younger, resembled his mother, being red-haired, blue-eyed, sparkling and rather naughty; he was being slightly naughty as usual. The steps excited him, and presently he snatched his hand from Lucy's and ran off to them. He seated himself proudly on each top step as he encountered it, to the sad detriment of his white home-made sailor suit, then jumping up with a ringing laugh sprang down to the pavement. Unfortunately the steps, though they remained few in number, increased in depth with the gradient of the terrace.

"He'll fall, Mother," observed Ned mildly.

Lucy sighed. Why was Harry always so *naughty*? The soiling of the sailor suit, washed and ironed only yesterday, was bad enough, but the ridicule of the boy's performance in the eyes of all Annotsfield—passers-by were actually laughing—vexed Lucy's proud spirit. She took a step forward, intending to pursue the naughty but dearly loved boy, remembered that it was not wise for her to run, since she was pregnant with her third child (me), and instead urged her elder son :

"Stop him, Ned."

Ned obediently rushed after his brother.

Too late, alas. Harry, leaping down yet another pair of steps, miscalculated their depth, tripped and fell. Never slow to express his feelings, he howled. A lady in an elegantly cut walking dress of fine indigo worsted—trust Lucy to perceive its quality—with a handsome cameo brooch and a superlative hat of spiky dark blue satin bows, was moving with dignity down the dentist's long path. She hastened her step, tucked her silver-cornered purse under one arm and lifted Harry to his feet. Lucy, hastening her steps as much as she dared, cried : "Thank you !" in mingled gratitude and resentment, and found herself face to face with her cousin.

"Lucy !"

"Kate !"

"We have not seen each other for a long time, Lucy." Kate's voice was dry, but shook.

"We live up the valley now, I don't often come into Annotsfield," panted Lucy.

"Why should we not be friends now, Lucy. All that old quarrel is over long ago. It was foolish. No doubt I was to blame. I was young. Let us be friends now, Lucy. You have two fine boys. I too have a son."

She looked towards the road. An open landau drawn by a fine chestnut horse and driven by a coachman in dark green livery, with a cockade in his hat, stood at the kerb. In it sat a boy. A year older than Ned, probably; fairish and solid, scowling a little but bright-eyed.

"The image," thought Lucy, "of his father, I don't doubt."

At this moment there uncurled itself from beneath the hind wheels of the landau, a dog. A huge, tall, sleek, smooth white Dalmatian, its sinewy body neatly spotted here and there in black. It came slowly towards Kate, stepping delicately, holding its long tapering tail stiffly aloof. Another similar animal followed. These "coach dogs", as they were then called, were at that time regarded in Annotsfield as the summit token, the very hallmark, of wealth.

"Let us be friends now, Lucy," Kate was murmuring.

But the Dalmatian was the last straw.

"No !" cried Lucy. "Never ! You made me bitterly unhappy in my young time, Kate. I am happy now. Don't come and spoil it all. I don't want you now."

"True. We do not need each other now," said Kate, very quiet and cold. She smiled, nodded, and moved away towards her carriage.

In fact, both women lied.

Lucy was a happy wife, loving and loved. Her sons were healthy. Edward, at her appeal, had given up playing rugby after losing a few teeth in a scrum, and settled down to be a steady married man. Her mother was never ill. Her beloved father had lately been showing some deterioration in heart and chest, but not more than was to be expected in a man of his age; his wife nursed him very precisely, and suitable specialists called in gave only mild and distant warnings. (They were wrong there, as it turned out, for Thomas Hallam died a few years after I was born, living just long enough to let me know him.) But Lucy was not yet worried by this possibility; being strong physically herself, she was not apt to foresee ill-health. No; the only thing that worried her was the state of the textile trade, which at that time was going up and down in prosperity as usual. Or rather, perhaps —to be honest—there were two things that worried her; the state of the textile trade, and Edward's lack of skill with money.

Everybody in the West Riding knew that Edward Randal was highly skilled as regards cloth. Oh yes, he knew cloth thoroughly, fleece to worsted. And was honest—almost too honest for his own good. But money bored him. Of a careless, generous disposition, somehow he could not *bother* with money. As long as old Sykes lived, all was well; Edward found the old man tiresome, finicking, pernickety, fussy, and hated the scoldings he gave his young partner every month. But everything was correct and in order. Edward and Lucy lived in a small but comfortable house in the village up the valley from Annotsfield. The hills, rocky, steep, purple with heather in autumn, towered around them and the young couple walked them eagerly; the rocky beck sparkled at the bottom of the field. They were not rich, but not poor; their income was steady, for old Sykes paid Edward a salary; the children were all one could wish.

But then old Sykes died. Edward was left to manage the firm. He enjoyed being his own master. But now not only his wife and children, his mother and one still unmarried sister, but old Sykes' widow and unmarried daughter, depended on his skill.

Then came the awful incident of the closed drawer. Ned was three months old when it occurred. A man from the village came to the door one afternoon to bring some raspberry canes ordered by Edward. Not having quite enough loose cash to pay him, and Edward being not yet returned from the mill, Lucy skipped blithely across the room to Edward's desk, where she often saw him inserting and removing papers. She pulled open the relevant drawer. It was full of unpaid bills.

Lucy, horrified, white and gasping, sank to a chair. Her face was so terrible that Baby Ned, frightened, set up a long loud howl. Lucy with some skill used this outburst as an excuse. Joggling Ned to ensure that his wail continued, she urged the raspberry man to call at the mill for his payment since Baby was in such a trying mood.

The scene between Lucy and Edward on Edward's return home was extremely painful. Lucy, daughter of a meticulously honest Hallam, sobbed and demanded to know how Ned's father could disgrace Ned so. Edward, bitterly ashamed, wept too, but somehow conveyed without uttering it his conviction that he never could manage money. Accounts, he said, were a torture no cloth man could endure. He did not, to be truthful, really understand them.

"At Cloughs' I never had anything to do with money," he lamented.

From that moment the Randal household never ran up a

bill. Lucy never bought anything she could not immediately pay for. She economised, she scraped; she did her own housework, she made her own dresses; she stitched the boys' sailor suits herself. So far, so good. The household was free of the slightest reproach. But what about the mill? Once, things grew so muddled there that she actually had to turn to her father for help.

"Ought you help Edward, Tom? Will he ever keep everything straight? Think of ourselves a bit, will you?" objected Hannah as they went to bed that night.

"I encouraged Edward to marry Lucy, so I must stand by it," returned Hallam, calm as usual.

"Well—"

"Edward is just a bit too soft, that's all. He's as honest as the day, but a bit too soft."

"I agree. But—"

"And nobody could be a better husband to our daughter."

"Well, that's true," yielded Hannah, warming a little.

"Or a better father to our grandchildren."

"Ha!" exclaimed Hannah, rolling over to smother her vexation. "The children are certainly lovely."

"Well, then."

"Very well, but don't land us in the poorhouse in our old age."

'I won't. Hannah," began Hallam very quietly: "I intend to buy that house they live in, Edgecote, and put the deeds in Lucy's name. Then they'll always have a roof over their heads."

"That's good, Tom, that's good. Yes, it's a good idea, is that. But don't ever tell Edward or Lucy, or those deeds will be in the bank as security for some overdraft of Edward's, before you know where you are."

"You're right. Perhaps I'd better put the deeds in your name."

"And do you think I could hold out against Lucy if she

wanted to use them? Don't put me in a position to have a family quarrel over a house! If I own the house, Edward and Lucy will hate me. If I'm poorly off, Edward will slave to see me put right."

"You like Edward more than you say."

"He's a good husband to our Lucy. Couldn't be kinder. That's what counts with a woman in wedlock, they say."

"Ah," sighed Hallam mildly.

But now at this moment when Lucy and Kate met, ten years after they married, Edward's affairs were in rather a muddle again. This time it was not his fault. The United States had slapped on a tariff to protect their own nascent textile industry, and textile imports from England dropped by more than half. The whole of the West Riding was therefore in trouble. Large firms like Cloughs' scowled, gritted their teeth, and lowered salaries and dividends to weather the storm. Smaller firms closed weaving sheds, and some firms staggering in difficulties went bankrupt.

"They say grass will grow in the streets of Bradford," said Lucy to her father, her voice shaking in spite of her efforts to be calm.

"It's a bad time but it will pass. The effects of tariffs never last very long," said Hallam. "The price inside the tariff wall soon rises to equal the price of the imports."

"I don't understand any of that," said Lucy impatiently. "Edward is worried to death, father. He can't eat or sleep. If you saw him!"

"I'll have a word with your bank manager," said Hallam.

He was doing precisely that at this moment, and Lucy was to call at the Hallam home for a midday meal to hear the result. What with this anguish of suspense, and the on-coming of this third child, unwanted, expensive, and so late, Lucy was in a state of acute nervous tension. The sight of Kate, so handsome and elegant in her expensive dress, with her landau and coachman and above all that odious Dog—

55

it just could not be borne. She had never needed Kate so much. It was too humiliating. It was all Edward's fault. For Edward's sake she could not bear it. Accordingly she rejected Kate's proffered friendship furiously, crying: "No! Never!"

They parted.

Kate, as her dress, her carriage and above all her Coach Dog showed, was not harassed by financial troubles. The recession had not affected the great Clough firm uncomfortably as yet, and at Clough Lea money seemed to abound pretty much as usual. Nor was Kate anxious about her offspring's physique. Her one son, Benjamin Garrett Clough, was in solid, not to say blooming, health. But she had trouble of another kind. Garrett was Ben's father's name, and Ben's son was named after him.

"I should like Milner for a second name, Ben," Kate had said the day after the child's birth, in the tone of a woman accustomed to loving acquiescence from her husband.

"I don't love old Josh so much I want to enshrine him in my son's name," said Ben unexpectedly. He paused and continued: "He gave me some very peevish looks just before we got engaged, Kate. So did you, by the way."

It was Kate's cue for a loving response, especially as she admitted to herself that she had indeed been slightly peevish on the afternoon of Ben's proposal. But she was vexed by "my son" from her husband in relation to a joint product, and by his depreciation of her father; besides, she had not forgiven Garrett for his bad behaviour at her wedding reception, when he became so drunk and noisy that he had to be persuaded to leave. Her tone was therefore not quite mild as she said, though she was careful to laugh as she spoke:

"Better my father's name than yours."

"Who says so?" retorted Ben. "I'm fond of my father. My grandfather spoiled my father by being too strict with him."

"Something spoiled him, certainly," said Kate, still laughing.

"Now, Kate," Ben rebuked her, his tone unusually heavy. "We won't do the same with our Ben. I mean that, Kate."

Now at last, just a little too late—it was their first open tiff—it occurred to the surprised Kate that when her husband spoke in that tone it might be best not to thwart him. Accordingly, young Benjamin Garrett was baptised as such and was not strictly disciplined; indeed one might say he was not disciplined at all. Any efforts Kate made in that direction were at once nullified by Ben, for if his son cried demandingly:

"Need I go to bed now, Father?"

Ben at once replied: "No!" and added: "Why do you bother him so, Kate? You're too fond of your own way. Let the child alone."

This sort of thing was the source of many small disagreements, which only needed a slightly increased acrimony to become quarrels. The sharper tone was provided presently by the habit Ben developed of coming home late at night, slightly drunk. Far from being softly welcoming on these occasions, for that was not her disposition, Kate was shocked and disgusted, and said so. Ben's excuse was always that he had been drinking with James, or Fred, or Charlie. These were names new to Kate, for it seemd Ben had given up playing rugby shortly after his marriage—or perhaps the local rugby team had given up Ben, on account of growing obesity and "lack of puff", as Annotsfield said. Kate, out of pride eager enough to clear him of fault, threw the blame of the glass-too-many on these new companions, and urged Ben to give them up. Ben thereupon snapped:

"You want me to give up all my friends, do you?"

"Of course not! I've never asked you before—"

"What about Edward? You choked him off pretty neatly, didn't you?"

"No, I did not."

"I couldn't have him for my best man, choose how."

"That was Lucy's fault."

"You were jealous of Lucy."

"I was *not* jealous of Lucy."

"There's two opinions about that."

"But what could I be jealous of Lucy *about* ?"

"An interesting question."

"Don't bait me like that, Ben Clough!" cried Kate, crimsoning as she lost her temper.

"Now we see the Milner temper in full display. Or perhaps your mother's?"

"What about *your* temper, Ben?"

"What, indeed!" shouted Ben, and uttering some oaths which in those days were regarded as an insult to a woman, he flung out of the room, slamming the door.

As the years went by and Ben became more used to, and therefore less struck by, Kate's beauty, his responses to her taunts became coarser and louder, and hers to his became shriller and keener. Mrs Clough, unable to bear their increasing bitterness, retreated to the South Coast, thus removing one check on their battles. Then old Mr Clough died. Garrett Clough, perhaps hoping for reinstatement, returned to Annotsfield for his father's funeral and showed a disposition to make his home there. Ben, wisely or not, kept his father out of the mill by bringing in a cousin to make up any of his own deficiencies. But Garrett Clough's presence in the house brought an air of dissipation which Kate could not endure, though Ben seemed almost to welcome his father's presence, so long as he kept out of the mill.

"Turn him out of the house or I'll leave you."

"*You*'ll leave *me* ! You've turned very moral of a sudden," sneered Ben.

"And why not? I'm your wife, think on."

Ben gave a jeering laugh.

58

The cousin made strong representations to Ben, for Garrett too often "dropped in", and Garrett soon left for London. But about this time it began to be said in Annotsfield that Ben Clough was going the same way as his father. Wine—and unfortunately women, too.

"Why do you stand it, Kate?" urged Joshua. "Put up a fight, lass. Go to Mrs Clough in the south."

"I have a son," said Kate coldly.

She had become very quiet and cold of late, and her displays of temper were nowadays rare. Annotsfield grew almost sorry for her. Presently it began to be rumoured that things at Clough Mills were not just as perfect as they had been of old. Ben knew cloth up to a point, of course, though not like his grandfather. But he seemed not to care, and so grew careless. As for the cousin, he was not really a textile man.

"Well, they've a long way to go, have Cloughs, before they're in the red."

"True. Some people have all the luck."

If only Edward had not left Clough Mills, reflected Kate, at first not very seriously, but later with increasing anguish and remorse. She had nothing definite against the managing cousin, except that he was tactless and irritated Ben. But if only Edward had been in his place, if only . . . how different everything would be. Then she began to dream that Edward might return. How it could be effected she could not imagine; but she imagined clearly the results of such a return : Ben happy with his old friend; abandoning his new dissipated acquaintance, giving up drink, staying at home; the two couples, Ben and Kate, Edward and Lucy, sitting peacefully side by side in front of a blazing Clough Lea hearth. Yes, if Edward returned everything might yet be well. Ben would reform, the mill return to its former perfection. If she could only make up the quarrel with Lucy ! How ? She had no idea. She did not even know where Lucy lived, nowadays. No doubt she could find out from Mr Hallam, through her father. But what a humiliation, to make such an enquiry! No, she could not bring herself to such abasement. She just dreamed, and hoped. Given the blessing of the chance meeting, she tried for a reconciliation. But old sins have long shadows, and proud Lucy refused.

The Clough-Hallam story continued for quite a long period after this meeting, for life goes on and actions continue to produce results, sometimes even to the third and fourth generations.

Thomas Hallam, as I said, died a few years after I was born. The property and investments he bequeathed to Lucy, though by Clough standards contemptibly small, were just enough to see the Hallams through the American tariff crises. Old Mrs Hallam, my grandmother, came to live with us. This was not a very comfortable arrangement, as Hannah and Lucy Hallam were both too spirited for their mutual comfort, and my father, Ned and myself, though we loved Grandfather Hallam, had no great fondness for Grandmamma. Fortunately, however, Grandmamma Hallam took a fancy to Harry, that lively spirited, undaunted boy, who teased her and made impertinent jokes to her, and read the newspaper to her and brought her Doncaster butterscotch, in a way she enjoyed.

(On Ned and myself devolved the more onerous tasks of providing her with library books and on myself the caps I have before referred to; we served her faithfully enough but she found us too meek for her taste.)

The Great War came upon us; Ned volunteered, was taken instantly into the army, and—as so often, alas, happened with the best of our youth—was killed before the year was out. Harry likewise presently enlisted, but being younger never actually reached France. Grandmamma Hallam, her hair, though slightly faded, still red to the last, died; at which event, I am sorry to say, all of us except Harry rejoiced. The post-war period brought prosperity for a while to the textile trade; we quietly flourished. Then the slump came. Harry now ran the mill admirably and with immense gusto, and pulled it through after some agonising but daring brinkmanships; he married a nice girl and had a son. Then presently the General Strike struck us a fearful blow.

It was during the year 1926, and in the very days of the strike, that Joshua Milner died. In Annotsfield it was said that the anguish of the strike killed him. As to this, I do not know, but believe it to be well possible; such a stubborn rejection of his hopes and plans, such total opposition to his will, might well have set up a stroke, as these occlusions were called in those days. On the afternoon after Joshua's death, my father and I were sitting miserably together in our front room—the mill was closed, so there was no work for him to go to—when the telephone rang, and immediately after answering it my mother came into the room.

"Harry wants me to go down there," said she.

We all knew that this delicately cryptic announcement referred to the imminence of labour for Harry's wife, who was, as we said in those days, for the second occasion, "near her time".

"Will you come with me, Rose?" said my mother.

Her tone was less assured than was customary with her, and when I looked at my father I guessed why. His face was pale and drawn, and for a moment the horrifying thought crossed my mind that if the strike could kill Joshua Milner, it might kill my father too.

"No—I think I'll just stay here this afternoon," I said.

My mother nodded agreement, gave a troubled glance at my father and left. A few moments later we heard her close the front door and step briskly down our gravel path. My father and I were left alone together. I pretended to read; my father tried to smoke a pipe.

After a time he gave up this attempt, and springing up from his chair began to pace up and down the room.

"It's no good, it's no good," he muttered. "It's no good, Rose. Probably nobody will ever know. Besides I think Ben knows already. It wouldn't do any good to tell. Your mother could triumph—but what good would it do her? Or she might be distressed. Make her even more bitter, perhaps. If the names are all right in the will, everything will be all right. If not, I don't see what they can do."

He gazed at me in piteous appeal.

"I don't know, father," I began—I was about to say: "what you're talking about," but it struck me that this sounded impertinent and unsympathetic, so I substituted stiffly—"to what you refer."

My father stared at me.

"She's not his wife," he said. "Ada, I mean. Not legally, you know. And so Kate is not his legal daughter."

"What!" I exclaimed. I was so dumbfounded and horrified that I really could not think of anything to say. "It can't be!"

"Yes, it is. Ada was a girl in his mill, very handsome, and Joshua—well, I suppose he got her with child," said my poor father, blushing with agony at this, in those days unheard-of, communication to a daughter. "His first wife had a couple of miscarriages, and then she was expecting again, and ill, and Joshua sent her off to the south coast—he Packed Her Off to the South Coast," cried my father, suddenly almost shouting in his indignation, "leaving your grandfather Hallam in charge of the mill, of course. But the poor thing didn't die quick enough, so Joshua couldn't marry Ada before Kate was born. It was more than two years when he came back to live in Annotsfield, you know, and when he came he brought Ada as his wife and Kate as their baby girl. But he couldn't marry her in time, you know."

"But do you think Grandfather Hallam knew about this?" I stammered.

"Of course he did!" shouted my father. "He just kept his mouth firmly shut and married Joshua's sister Hannah, so it was all in the family, so to speak. A family secret which of course they all kept."

The hint of a slight tinge of possible moral blackmail by Grandfather Hallam in this situation disturbed me; I dismissed it at once, for I knew my grandfather's character. But would Joshua have felt equally secure? Would the marriage of the nobody Thomas Hallam to the sister of the rich Joshua Milner have been accompanied without any pressure? Yes, I thought so; for they loved each other. All the same, I sought reassurance.

"Did he ever mention it to you—Grandfather Hallam, I mean?"

"No. Never. Your Grandfather Hallam," said my father, calming, "was a man of steel will and perfect integrity. He would never breathe a word to anyone, I am sure. Your grandmother certainly never knew."

"How do you know, then?"

"Garrett Clough told me."

"Garrett Clough?" I was stupefied. "But when?"

"My dear, by one of life's little ironies—a great one, in this case—it was on the very night of Ben and Kate's wedding. Garrett Clough got drunk at the reception and old Mr Clough practically threw him out and he wandered round the Annotsfield pubs and finished up at the Station, on his way to catch a London train. Of course, he missed one, and then some kindly porter pushed him out on the platform, and I was just walking along—we were coming back from Blackpool, you know; it was an excursion train and there was a considerable crowd and I became separated from the Hallams, and here was Garrett Clough clinging to my arm and sobbing on my shoulder. Of course I urged him to pull himself together and all that sort of thing, and eventually I managed to push him into the London express which came in on the other side of the platform, and he hung out of the window shouting at me. 'I've plenty to weep for!' he shouted. 'My son's just married a bastard, the daughter of a—' I won't use such a word to you, Rose," said my poor father. "But he meant Ada, you know. Oh yes, he meant Ada. And the moment I began to think about it, of course, I saw it all."

"But how did Garrett Clough know?"

"Trust Garrett to know Annotsfield scandal! He made plenty himself. And I reckon he had told Ben at the reception. He was just in the mood to do it."

"Told Ben! But surely Uncle Joshua must have told Ben when Ben and Kate first planned to be married?"

"Joshua tell Ben! Not he. Ben might have duffed, as we say in Yorkshire; he might have called the marriage off. I don't doubt," continued my father in a kinder tone, "that your Great-uncle Joshua married Ada when he could. But it would be later, and in some registrar's office in some far-off southern place, or London, you know, where nobody up here would hear of it. But a marriage after Kate was born wouldn't make her legitimate, would it?"

For in those days such was indeed the harsh law.

"It's a terrible story, father," said I.

"Aye. It all depends on Joshua's will now, doesn't it? If he's *named* Ada and Kate as his beneficiaries—Catherine Mary Clough, you know—that'll be all right. But if he's just said "wife" and "daughter", they may be in for a lot of trouble. Especially Kate. I don't know enough law to say. In any case the daughter matter may come out and be talked about in Annotsfield, because nowadays newspapers publish wills."

"Uncle Joshua was far too shrewd not to tie it all up tightly," I said. "It's right Kate should have her father's money." My tone was a trifle sardonic here, I fear. I meant entirely what I said, and would not have assisted to deprive Kate of Joshua's wealth for anything in the world, but per-

64

haps I could not altogether resist a qualm of irritation in my
heart. I knew too well the troubles lack of capital could cause.
A lack which Kate would never know. Would the fact of my
own legitimate birth enable me to subdue this qualm more
easily? I am ashamed to have to say, yes. But did I want
to be Joshua's daughter? No! Not at any price. "Let us be
thankful it has nothing to do with us, father," I said.

"You think not?"

"I do."

"I don't want to tell anybody. It's not the sort of thing
I care to do. I've kept silent all these years. I've kept it from
your mother—I didn't want to upset her. I didn't even tell
Ned. But now I just wonder about Ben's son."

"What does it matter?" I thought with youthful contempt.
But what matters is too often what people believe to matter.
Still, my father's thinking of Ned as his first trust helped me,
for what would Ned, our dearest and our best, have thought
of this wretched tale? I knew well enough, for I had loved
my brother Ned.

"If you had known about Kate's birth when you were
friends with Ben, father, would you have told Ben?"

"No!" said my father with emphasis. "Of course not!
Sure to make him unhappy. Might have spoiled his life. I
was too much his friend."

"Then be a friend to him still."

My father sank down in his chair, looking relieved.

"I will," he said.

Yes, I thought, all those concerned had in their own way
loved each other. *"I've known a hundred kinds of love,"* I
remembered : *"All make the loved one rue."*

"You're a good girl, Rose," said my father.

"I try to be your daughter," said I.

The door opened and my mother came in. She looked so
distressed that my father at once went to her.

"Pamela?" he queried anxiously, naming Harry's wife.

65

"No. She's all right. It was a false alarm," said my mother. She paused, then burst out: "It's Ben and Kate. Harry says they're going to part."

"What!"

"It's all over Annotsfield, Harry says. Now Joshua's gone, Kate and her mother are to live in the south somewhere together."

"What about young Ben?"

"He'll stay with his father in Annotsfield."

"He's got that big mill to run soon," said my father, rather grim. "Well, he's a solid, gruff chap, from all I hear, is young Ben. Knows his own mind and sticks to it, like old Joshua. If he takes my advice he'll throw that cousin out, first thing. People don't like that man. He's not West Riding."

"If he takes *my* advice, he'll throw his drunk of a father out too," said my mother, a good deal more grim.

Jealousy is cruel as the grave, I thought.

"Nay, Lucy!" my father reproached her, shocked.

"Well, it's not our affair, thank goodness," I said hastily.

"You know nothing about it, Rose," said my mother with dignity.

You will understand, I hope, why I made no attempt to correct her.

LEILA

1900

E DWARD M ILNER , J UNIOR , was nine years old
when, at the beginning of the century, his sister Leila was
born.

It was all very uncomfortable at the time. Lying in bed
asleep with his teddy-bear snug at his side—a childhood relic,
a very fine large animal with thick fawn fur, which his
father had brought him from London—Edward had been
awakened several nights in succession by harsh sounds from
his parents' bedroom next door. Voices? Yes, Edward
drowsily thought so—but that could hardly be, for the sounds
were swift and angry, as if his father and mother were
quarrelling, what Annie in the kitchen called "having a row",
and this was most unlikely, as his father and mother adored
each other, everyone knew that. Edward remembered his
Aunt Audrey, his uncle Gerald's wife, once drawling in her
rather acid tones : "*I* shouldn't like it if *my* husband travelled
abroad and left me as much as Claire's does." Of course
Uncle Gerald was not the brother of Edward's mother, just
her cousin, so he was not a real uncle, one just called him
so out of politeness; he was rather handsome, very fair, and
Aunt Audrey was, to tell the truth, rather sallow and faded,
so she might well feel a little catty towards his mother, reflected Edward. But that wasn't what he was thinking about.
What was he in fact—oh, yes; it was his father's reply.
"Claire has no need to worry," said his father stiffly, looking

aside to conceal his feelings, while his mother, exhaling smoke down her nostrils, lazily, almost triumphantly, smiled.

Of course Edward's mother—she never called him Ted, as she did his father—was very beautiful. Very. With wonderful thick golden hair which gleamed in the light, and large brilliant grey eyes, she always attracted a great deal of attention, especially in the evening, in the elegant pale evening dresses she wore. Yes, it was generally accepted in the Milner household that Mummy was superior in looks to practically everybody else in the world. Her name before her marriage had been Lacy, and it seemed there had been Earls of that name in the West Riding a long time ago.

"But surely, Claire, you're not suggesting that you are descended from those old chaps?" said his father, laughing.

"How should I know?" said Edward's mother, smiling. "The name's the same."

"Well, Milner is a good old West Riding name too," said his father. "There were Milners in Hudley in 1526—I've seen a copy of the Will of them."

"But they weren't earls, Ted," said his mother gently.

"No—they owned a mill by the river, ground oats and fulled cloth. They were in the cloth trade," said Ted Milner, "like me. I'm content to follow them."

"You're wonderful, Ted," drawled Claire; she turned her beautiful face up to his and he stooped and kissed it.

Of course, even a child like Edward could hear that Claire Lacy sounded better than Ted Milner. And though Ted Milner was not an ugly man, he couldn't of course compare in looks with his beautiful wife. Ted was of middle height, sturdy, with broad shoulders, mid-brown in an ordinary way, with a firm jaw and a pleasant smile. The Milners appeared to be rich, or at least well-off, and this, so at least Annie said—Annie had been Ted's nurse when he was a child, it seemed—was entirely due to Ted's efforts. Edward took this for granted; of course his father was rich, if that was the right thing for a father to be. Naturally his father was everything he ought to be. A father ought to be strong, sturdy, with a plain name and a beautiful wife. Edward adored his mother and loved his father with his whole heart.

It was lovely when sometimes, in his school holidays, he rode off in the car beside his father down to the mill. His mother stood on the steps of the Hall and waved goodbye to them as they drove away, and Edward felt proud and happy.

Better still when all three Milners drove off together to some entertainment—a circus visiting Hudley, the sailing club on a reservoir up on the moors, the golf club where Edward walked round the holes with his father.

Best of all when Edward and his mother went to the station to meet his father on his return home from one of the business trips he was always making in order to sell his cloth. It was tremendously exciting to see the signal go down for the train, see the train come round the corner in the far distance, watch it grow larger and larger and finally steam into the platform, enormous. Edward felt quite pale with excitement at this crucial moment and even his mother looked a trifle wan as if she felt excited too. Then his father came down the steps from a first-class coach and walked steadily towards them, smiling, and then he took them both strongly in his arms. That was splendid.

So that now to imagine that his father and mother were quarrelling was really quite absurd.

All the same, some odd things seemed to be happening in the house. His mother began to look pale and almost haggard, so that her beauty was decidedly diminished. His father appeared cross and abrupt, and two vertical lines began to show down the centre of his forehead, giving him an angry and resentful air. They talked very little, so that meals were eaten almost in silence. Then there came an afternoon during Edward's Easter holidays. His father being at the mill as usual, his mother said she had a headache, and sharply bidding Edward leave her, went to her bedroom to lie down. The rain was pouring down outside and Edward had finished his library book, so he wandered slowly along the landing after his mother's rebuff, wondering what to do. Observing a little-used bedroom door standing open, he strolled in for lack of any better occupation, and saw the single bed made up and his father's hairbrushes lying on the dressing-table, his father's dressing-gown hanging on the hook at the back of the door.

The shock was very great. He did not know what this separation of his parents meant, but knew it was something awful.

Sure enough, next morning Annie came to him before he was up, and said he must rise at once, as they had to catch a train at half-past nine.

"Where are we going?" whispered Edward. His sense of disaster was so strong, he dared not speak aloud.

"To your grandmother's."

Dazed and frightened, Edward did not even venture to ask which of his grandmothers was meant. He did not care for either of them much. Mrs Lacy was handsome and elegantly dressed, with beautiful white hair, but there was never much to eat in her flat, and she was rather hard and a bit of a liar. Mrs Milner was a good deal older; she always gave one plenty to eat and she was not sarcastic, but her iron grey hair, her clothes and her morals were all decidedly grim. They were both widows, and lived in widely separated seaside resorts on the south coast.

Edward's father, looking really very ill, drove Edward and Annie to the station, and kissed Edward goodbye with a kind of despairing warmth, as if he never hoped to see him again. Edward's mother was not visible that morning, and Edward dared not ask for her. In the uneasy rush his bear was left behind.

It turned out that Mrs Milner was to be his hostess. She met her guests at the station, and though looking extremely unhappy, greeted them very warmly. Her house in Southstone was a large old-fashioned affair, well situated near the sea, well appointed, well kept, with an old neat maid in the kitchen, who turned out to be Annie's sister. Annie was to stay at old Mrs Milner's to assist in the burden understood to be caused to the household by Edward's presence.

This was reassuring, for Edward was attached to Annie, and after a few days he settled down fairly well. The spring proved warm and the sea was a pleasure, often agreeably rough and with plenty of ships passing up and down. The beach was pebbly, but Edward was too old for a bucket-and-spade routine nowadays, as he told himself proudly. The holidays went, term-time approached; to Edward's surprise he learned he was not to return home yet, but stay in Southstone and go to school there. His grandmother told him that his mother was not well, and had been advised to spend some months in Switzerland.

"She's not *ill*?" said Edward, alarmed.

"Not very ill," said his grandmother in a constrained tone.

"Then why must she go to Switzerland?"

"Just a precautionary measure."

Edward felt that there was more behind this than he was told. He was disappointed about school, too, for he had had hopes of the junior football team in his Hudley school. Of course he was too firm in character to show his dismay. He held his head up and was ready to bark in north-country style at any boy who showed a lack of proper respect for him. But as it turned out this didn't prove necessary. The first lad he met was Jack Clarkson; they became friends at once and the friendship lasted for life.

A few days before Christmas his father turned up. He looked older than Edward remembered him, for his hair was quite plentifully streaked with grey. He had come to fetch

Edward home. Edward perceived at once that his grandmother opposed this. There were long arguments between
old Mrs Milner and her son, which ended abruptly whenever
Edward entered the room. Really grown-ups were extra-
ordinarily simple, quite foolish in fact, reflected Edward
impatiently, if they believed they could conceal happenings
of that kind from their children. Eventually his father won
the argument—his father usually won arguments; he was a
determined sort of man, thought Edward approvingly—and
the two set off on the long journey north together. Annie
had preceded them by a couple of days.

At first Ted Milner was cheerful. He seemed happy to
have his son with him and heaped small indulgences on him
—ice-cream and orange squash and comic papers. Edward
found this affection warming. He enjoyed lunching with his
father in the restaurant car, and felt very grown-up when
one or two men came and had a word with his father on
textile subjects. Ted introduced him : "This is my son,
Edward." The men, puffing comfortably at their cigars, said
in their deep Yorkshire voices : "Chip of the old block, eh?
He's the image of you, Ted. What's your name, sonny?"
It was all very pleasant.

But when the train entered Yorkshire and the first mill
chimneys began to appear, suddenly cheerfulness fell from
his father's shoulders like a doffed coat. He looked not only
old but haggard, almost ill. Often he turned to Edward as
if about to speak, but as often turned away without saying
anything. Edward began to feel uneasy, chilled. What was
wrong? He gazed imploringly at his father, and suddenly,
when the train was actually puffing up the cutting towards
Hudley, Ted exclaimed roughly :

"You've got a little sister now, Edward."

Edward almost laughed with relief. Was that all? Did his
father really think that Edward, whose recent birthday had
brought him into double figures, knew nothing about women

having babies? Of course it was all a trifle vague as yet, Edward was not at all sure exactly what—or how—people were always squeamish about mentioning it, he knew—but still, a lot of fellows' mothers had babies. It was nothing to make a fuss about.

"What's her name?" he asked, putting the matter firmly on a practical basis.

"Leila."

Privately, Edward thought Leila rather a silly name. But girls were rather silly in many ways, he reflected; one just had to put up with it. He said no more on the matter.

It was dark when they got out of the train at Hudley, and Hudley always looked its best in the dark. The chains of lights shooting along the sides of the valleys and climbing laboriously up the dark hills—"diamonds on black velvet", somebody had once said in Edward's hearing, and he thought that a very good description—made beautiful patterns, and suddenly he found he had missed the West Riding terribly, and was terribly glad to be home. This feeling mounted and mounted as they drove towards the Hall, so that he actually ran into the drawing-room, which was very bright and warm with a glorious fire and a great many flowers, as usual, and when he saw his mother standing by the hearth, looking very beautiful if rather pale, he burst into tears and rushed to her and threw his arms round her waist and buried his head in her breast. His mother put her arms round him and kissed him and smoothed his hair and kissed him again, and her warmth and her lovely scent quite overcame him and he really quite sobbed. (It was disgraceful in a ten-year-old, he knew, but he simply could not help it.) His father prowled about the room, and it seemed to Edward, on raising for a moment his tear-stained face, that he saw tears standing in his father's eyes too.

"Where's the baby?" asked Edward hoarsely, wanting to recover his composure and be polite.

"Annie will show you, dear," said his mother, putting him gently aside.

So in a moment he found himself gazing at this small new being. She was asleep in her elegant cot. One tiny fist was stretched above her head, the other hand lay outside the white satin coverlet. To tell the truth, Edward was rather impressed. Those very tiny fingers, which now moved, curling and spreading, were remarkably accurate in design. The fair lashes lying on the clear round cheek—really they were rather pretty. Moved by an unexpected impulse, Edward gently inserted his forefinger into the tiny palm. The fingers closed round his, and Leila gave a very quiet, very sleepy, very tiny coo.

"Darling little thing! You're a darling, aren't you?" murmured Annie fondly, bending over the cot.

"She's not at all bad," said Edward in a grown-up masculine voice. "Prettier than most, I should say."

Annie laughed, and Edward condescended to smile.

In a postcard written to Jack about this time, he confirmed the opinion he had formed: "My new sister is a pretty little thing, as infants go," he said.

So now there were four in the Milner household. Edward's father, Edward's mother, Edward, Leila.

His father yielded to his mother in everything, went out of his way to provide her with the luxuries she loved, and showed the greatest tenderness and warmth to little Leila. He did not show extra tenderness to Edward, but then that was not necessary. Ted and Edward had always been close friends, and now it seemed as if they were in a kind of pleasant conspiracy together to make the lives of their women-folk as comfortable and happy as possible. Neither Claire nor Leila seemed to appreciate this quite as much as they might have done, Edward sometimes fleetingly reflected; his mother's smile was sometimes weary, her drawl sometimes cold. Women were like that, he supposed.

As for little Leila, who grew rapidly, she was a perfectly healthy and very beautiful child. She had lovely pale gold hair and gleaming dark blue eyes. As soon as she could walk she ran about all over the place, so that poor old Annie grew short of puff (as Edward phrased it to himself) running after her. For it must be admitted—Edward admitted it gravely— that Leila was rather a naughty little girl. When carried away to bed in Annie's arms, for instance, she was capable of hitting Annie quite hard about the face, so that the kind-hearted Edward was shocked. Also, she treated his old bear, which had been found in a cupboard and presented to her by Edward with some ceremony—he was far too old for it now, of course, but all the same the gift was a real sacrifice— with savage disrespect. (Its eyes fell out under her callous handling, its fur came off in patches.) As she grew older, when displeased she threw breakable objects to the floor and laughed at the sound of breakage. When rebuked, she ground her teeth, her beautiful little face became distorted with rage, her lovely eyes flashed fire.

"You mustn't be a naughty little girl, Leila," said Edward to her a few years later, when speech had been added to her powers of provocation. (She had been very rude to Aunt Audrey. "I don't like your dress as well as Mummy's," she had said. Considering that Uncle Gerald was not at all well-off, this was really rude.)

"I shall be naughty if I like," said Leila, tossing her beautiful head.

"People don't like naughty little girls," said the serious Edward.

"Yes, they do. I don't care anyway," said Leila.

The difficulty was that she was right. Guests to the house (except Aunt Audrey) were entranced by her beauty and her spirit. When Edward and his father took her out—always elegantly dressed and as it were polished to the nines—she invariably attracted admiring comment. She could put on the most charming manners when she had a mind, of course. When she raised those beautiful eyes and gazed softly at the speaker, or lowered her head modestly and gave a delicious shy smile, she was irresistible. Even Edward's school friends (except Jack) admired her, were eager to help her over fences or fetch a chair or ice-cream at prize-givings—any excuse to be able to touch her hand. After a while, when Edward had grown up a bit, this kind of universal courtship —or at least Leila's coquettish response to it—sometimes made him a trifle uneasy, but he did not allow himself to take it too seriously, for after all, Leila was still only a little girl.

Then one day, when he was strolling round the Hall grounds with Jack, who had come to stay with him in the holidays, they came upon Leila being kissed by one of his schoolmates behind the rhododendrons. It was a very fervid kiss, and the attitudes of the participants were fervid too. Edward was furious.

"Leave my sister alone!" he shouted, springing forward.

The lad who had been kissing, laughed. Edward hit him. The lad hit Edward. He was a good deal bigger than Edward, and things might have been unpleasant if Jack had not stepped between them and saying in a calm commanding tone: "Stop it, you two!" struck up their fists.

"I shan't stay to tea!" laughed the older boy, vanishing over the wall.

"Good riddance," called Jack after him cheerfully.

"Leila, that was very naughty, very naughty indeed," said Edward, seizing Leila's wrist and turning her towards him. "I'm shocked, I really am. What would Mother say if she knew?"

"She wouldn't care," said Leila. She snatched her wrist away and ran off towards the house.

There was something hard and ugly in her tone which distressed Edward.

"I must apologise to you, Jack," he said stiffly after a moment. "I'm sorry you were let in for that."

"Oh, come off it, Edward," returned Jack. They turned and strolled away from the house. "She's right, though, isn't she?" he added after a pause.

"How do you mean?"

"Your mother wouldn't care."

It was a moment of severe shock, and Edward came out of that shock with memories supporting Jack's statement swarming in his head like angry bees. Yes, it was true; his mother did not care what happened to Leila. In fact, she was beastly to her. He recalled how rarely it happened that the four Milners went out together. If something suitable for children were planned, Claire was tired and stayed at home; if the excursion were designed for grown-ups, Edward was pronounced just old enough to go, but Leila was far too young. Edward recalled his mother's angry tone when she summoned the child to have a thread removed from her dress or a collar turned down, her ungentle gestures when she brushed down Leila's skirt or pulled up a sock. He remembered that once when Aunt Audrey had drawled: "How did you come to choose Leila's name, Claire?" his mother had replied: "Oh, I just turned over the pages of a book of names and stuck in a pin." Leila, her face dark with rage and grief, had rushed from the room. Ever since Leila's birth Edward had been regarded as too old a boy to receive a goodnight visit and kiss from his mother in his bedroom. Now he thought he saw that the cessation of this custom for him was just an excuse to omit Leila from it too.

He felt choked, and his heart pained him. Then came a melting rush of compassion.

"Poor Leila," he said. "It's no wonder she's a bit—"

"No," agreed Jack gravely, nodding.

Edward was now in his mid-teens, and the time had come for him to go away to some large public school. Of course he went to the school where Jack boarded, and they were very happy together. Edward wrote a joint letter to his father and mother every week, as was the custom; he also wrote cards quite regularly to poor little Leila.

Coming North in his first holidays at the big school, he was met at the station by his father, who told him of a party for Edward's friends which was being planned. Amongst the guests' names occurred that of the boy found kissing Leila. Edward demurred.

"I hope you're not going to turn snobbish and forget your old Hudley friends, Edward," said his father.

"No, of course I'm not," said Edward. He thought the matter over, decided against broaching the subject of Leila, and said: "Well, he annoyed me but I suppose I'd better forgive him."

"Never forgive anyone, Edward," said his father sharply.

"What do you mean?" said Edward, astonished.

"Forgiveness is unbearable to the forgiven."

Edward did not know what to say, so very wisely said nothing. The party went off as arranged. Leila wore a pale yellow frock and looked brilliant. She vanished from time to time and Edward had his suspicions but let them go. She was really *very* pretty, and that sort of thing was done nowadays.

It was in the next Christmas holidays that Edward came home to find old Annie in bed.

"The poor old thing has broken her leg," explained his father. "You'd better go up to see her straight away, Edward. She's been asking for you. Come down to the mill afterwards, if you like. But, Annie—" he lowered his voice—"she hasn't much time left, I'm afraid."

Edward was disappointed not to drive off with his father after lunch down to the mill, for this had become one of his regular holiday pleasures, but he readily admitted Annie's prior claim, and went cheerfully upstairs to visit her.

Her appearance shocked him. She looked small, shrunken, her face all yellow and fallen in, her grey hair wild and tangled.

"Well, Annie," he said, sitting on the bed and taking her hand, in which the pulse laboured jerkily, within his own. "What do you mean by being in bed for my holidays, eh?"

"Never mind that, Master Edward. I want to talk to you serious," whispered Annie.

"I'm listening, Annie," said Edward soberly.

"I want you to promise me you'll be good to Miss Leila."

"Why, of course I will."

"Nobody else will. Your mother hates her."

Edward looked away, embarrassed, unable to force a denial.

"You know why, don't you?"

"No, I don't think I do," said Edward.

"You're old enough to understand, now. She's your father's love-child, that's why."

"Nonsense! It's not true!" gasped Edward.

"Yes, love, it's true," said Annie sadly.

"Do you mean my father has admitted it to you?"

"No, no. But don't you remember when I took you down to Southstone when you were a little boy? Your mother pretended to be ill and went off to Switzerland, and you were sent off to Southstone, to hide it all, you see. Then the baby was fetched and your mother brought it back to Hudley and pretended it was hers. To keep the family together. She forgave him, you see."

Edward groaned, remembering in anguish his father's saying: *Forgiveness is unbearable to the forgiven.* All was explained: the coldness in the house, his mother's hatred of Leila, his father's excessive yielding to his wife and continual acts of love to the child. For Edward's sake, to keep the family together, Claire had forgiven her husband's infidelity, taken its result into the family. Poor, poor Leila. His mother's action was saintly, but all the same, poor Leila. Edward's world, hitherto so safely based, in utter reliance, upon his father, cracked all round him, broke and sank into grey ashes.

"Not that I blame him altogether," mused Annie. "He's attractive to women, and your mother was always a rather cold piece."

"Don't, Annie, don't. It makes me sick," said Edward, turning aside.

"You'll understand it better when you're older."

"I don't think so." (It was an unbearable humiliation that the deception about his half-sister had been undertaken largely for his own benefit.)

"Anyway, I had to tell you, because of poor Miss Leila. Look after her, Master Edward. Being the daughter of a—a loose woman, you know—naturally she can't help being a bit wild."

"I'll try."

"She's your father's daughter, Master Edward. You've always been fond of your father."

"Yes, I have been fond of him," said Edward bitterly.

Every fibre of his body revolting against the action, he laid his hands on Annie's shoulders and tenderly kissed her cold and withered cheek.

Two days later she was dead.

Edward never entered his father's mill again. Jack was to become a solicitor in his father's practice, so Edward opted for this profession too. His father was hurt.

"I hoped you'd come in with me, Edward," he said. "There's a good living there. Pity to let it drop."

"You'd better take in old Higgins' son," muttered Edward, naming his father's admirable works manager.

"I don't want Higgins' son. I want my own."

If Edward had been a little older, at this point he might

have blurted out some comment about Leila, but he was too young yet to venture it, and said nothing.

"Well, do what you want, Edward," said his father wearily. "I'll go in for a merger, I think. There's your mother and Leila to be provided for. I must secure that."

"Yes," said Edward.

After this Edward in fact spent little time in his home. He missed the West Riding a good deal, but could not bear the Hall.

He and Jack went to Oxford together and did rather well there. Edward took all the necessary examinations and performed all the necessary procedures, and presently found himself a junior partner in the firm of Clarkson, Clarkson and Milner, solicitors, in Southstone. At this point he married Jack's sister, Dorothy, an extremely nice, honest, good, not especially pretty but very lovable and loyal girl with large brown eyes. Just then the first World War broke out. Jack and Edward were of course involved in it but came back alive; though Jack had lost an arm and Edward had a bad limp, they counted themselves lucky. Coming out of hospital, Edward discovered that both his grandmothers and his father had died of the influenza epidemic of 1918, so he went north to settle the family affairs.

The excellent family solicitor of the Milners, who was Edward's godfather, had already done this to Edward's perfect satisfaction, so that only his signature was required, but naturally Edward went through every detail carefully. The textile business had been sold on excellent terms, for the post-war boom was still in being, so there was plenty of money. Edward was, however, rather surprised by the terms of his father's will. The provision for his mother was just a trifle meagre, he thought, and given to her only for life; Leila fared rather better and the money was her own, but he himself was so very much the largest beneficiary that he felt embarrassed and ashamed. He coloured as he expressed this, stammering, for the family secret laid restraint on his tongue.

"There is a private communication for you from your father, Edward," said the solicitor drily.

He handed over an envelope addressed simply *Edward*, sealed rather portentously with a very large blob of red wax.

This obvious demand for secrecy made Edward dread what he should read within. The note was very short and said simply. *My dear son, Whatever you may feel, look after Leila. I rely on you. Father.*

Edward sprang up and paced the room. His heart was full of rage, humiliation, and—he could not help it—pity. He felt insulted, outraged; the very signature was an agony, for he recalled all too well that he had never called Ted Milner *father* since Annie's revelation. (He omitted any name, or said *sir*; the feeling implied by *father* had been killed by his father's other paternity.) And now here was his father making this pathetic appeal. He must have loved Leila's mother very much, thought Edward. *I rely on you.*

"Do you know what my father has written to me?" he demanded, standing before the solicitor's desk with a very stern look.

"No. And I shall not attempt to guess."

Of course the man, his father's close friend, must know the whole thing, reflected Edward angrily. With an effort he calmed himself and said stiffly:

"I shall do my best to comply with his request."

The solicitor bowed his head.

As it turned out, Edward's promise was more easily given than kept, for Leila proved a thorn in his side for years. He moved his mother and his half-sister to an agreeable old cottage on a hill slope outside Hudley, having first asked Claire whether she wished to keep Leila with her. A spasm of anger crossed his mother's still-beautiful face.

"I suppose I must," she said.

"I don't want to live with you," said Leila, tossing her head.

Edward took no notice of this petulance, merely observing that the girl's fair beauty, in the heavy mourning then thought proper, was more remarkable than ever.

Leila was sent to an excellent boarding-school, from which she ran away, journeying homeward by night with a lorry-driver and making no secret of this adventure. (Hudley was shocked to the core.) She was sent to another boarding-school, almost as good, which quite promptly asked that she should be removed as a bad influence, and to a third, which publicly expelled her. Each time, Edward travelled north to cope with the problem.

"What would you *like* to do, Leila?" he said heavily on the last occasion. "What do you *want* to do? Tell me, and I will help you."

"I want to go to London and have a good time," said Leila, laughing.

"I can't let you do that," said Edward gravely, looking at the quite exquisite face turned up to his.

Leila laughed and danced away.

"Why not let her go, Edward?" said his mother.

"She wouldn't be safe," said Edward. "We have a duty . . . I think she must say with you."

"She's been a trouble and a nuisance to me always," said his mother quickly in a very irritable tone. "I didn't want her, I never have, I should be glad to see her go. Your father——" She bit her lip and broke off.

Edward being what he was, the result of this speech was naturally that Edward took Leila home with him to South-stone. Dorothy, who like many daughters-in-law was not particularly fond of her mother-in-law, welcomed Leila from Mrs Milner's unkindness with open arms. But after a week she broke into tears and confessed to Edward that she could not bear Leila's presence any longer. Leila smoked (at her age!), she drank, she lay in bed in the mornings, she used far more cosmetics than Southstone thought allowable; worst of all, when playing with the Milners' little daughter, she excited her to such a wild pitch of enjoyment that the child became hysterical and could not eat or sleep.

"Leila," began Edward gravely.

"I know. I'm sorry, Edward," said Leila sweetly. "I know I'm a nuisance. Dorothy's done her best."

Leila went home to Hudley and began an art course at the Hudley Technical College, but was soon reported to be coming to London to attend a school of dancing. Edward went firmly up to London and after a good deal of trouble arranged that Leila should live in a students' hostel. She soon left this for a flat which she shared with two other girls. Edward went firmly up to London, but Leila looked so beautiful and for the first time so happy, in her leotard, that he gave her a little present (ten pounds) and left her where she was.

Of course this was not the end of Leila. In spite of her nice little income she often wrote and said she hadn't a bean left to pay the rent—Edward sent a cheque. She wrote and said she thought she was going to need an abortion—what did Edward advise? Edward went swiftly up to London and shouted at the young man concerned ("quite a nice young fellow, really," he confided to Dorothy, perplexed), so that a marriage ceremony was performed. Shortly after this Leila had a miscarriage (or said so) and lost the child; shortly after this she divorced her young husband—Edward went a great deal to London to get the divorce through. Then Leila married again without telling Edward—or did she just go to live with the man? Edward was never sure. She got a job with a ballet company, and threw it up, breaking her contract, and got another similar job, and lost that. Edward's legal training stood him in good stead through all her scrapes. At length, if Edward gave a sigh as he opened his letters at the breakfast-table, Dorothy would say mildly :

"Leila again, I suppose."

And presently even Edward's son and daughter would laugh :

"Aunt Leila again !"

"It all falls on you, dear," said Dorothy admiringly. She thought the way he managed the Milner affairs was simply marvellous.

For of course Leila was not the only snag in the quiet waters of Edward's happy life.

"Every family man has troubling responsibilities," he said soothingly to Dorothy. "If it were not so solicitors would be out of work."

His mother, for instance, often spent too much and got into debt. He thought of making her a regular additional allowance, but Jack was against this.

"You're too good, Edward. If you give her more, she'll just spend beyond it as before, and be no better off. Better pay what she owes at the end of every year."

It was good advice. Edward took it, but it meant he had to do the long railway journey to the north, rather often, which now that old Mr Clarkson was dead and the firm extremely busy because of its high repute, became rather too time-wasting.

Then there was Uncle Gerald, who got into a financial mess and went into a rather discreditable bankruptcy with his small wine-business. Since Gerald and Audrey had no children, Edward went north and settled it all up, and found enough money somehow for them to live on. Then Uncle Gerald went senile and had to be settled in a nursing home. Edward went north and attended to the matter. His mother became very petulant, demanding and fretful as the years passed by and her beauty faded; she had to accept paid companions, whom she frequently dismissed, sending Edward frantic telegrams for help in these recurring crises. Edward suggested that his aunt and his mother should live together, but they both hotly refused.

All this was becoming really tiresome, for Edward's lame leg grew painful when fatigued, when suddenly things took a brighter turn.

His mother died. Edward was ashamed to regard this as a boon, but could not help doing so. She had shown him little love and much grumbling during the past few years. Edward, remembering that he was the son of the man who had been unfaithful to her, could not think this unreasonable, but she was his mother and her indifference hurt him. Its absence was a relief.

Then, Leila appeared in Southstone, really, properly, indubitably and very successfully married. She brought her husband with her, and Edward saw at once that this time the marriage would be permanent. True, Leila's husband was a foreigner and a good deal older than Leila, but he was a banker, immensely rich, handsome in a sophisticated grey-at-the-temples style, and—above all—a man of iron will. It was obvious that Leila had met her match. Her elegant black frock and hat, her superb furs, her exquisite jewellery, enhanced her fair beauty almost beyond belief.

"This is my dear brother, Edward," she said.

Edward was pleased by this tribute and shook hands with the financier warmly.

"I'm off your hands now, Edward. André will look after me."

"But yes," said André with emphasis, and it was clear that he meant it.

The very next day a telegram came from Aunt Audrey saying that Uncle Gerald had passed away. Edward of course went north, arranged the funeral and settled his uncle's meagre affairs. Sitting with his aunt by the fire in the evening before he left for the south, he said to her :

"Why don't you come to Southstone, aunt? I could find you a nice little flat. Dorothy would help you to get settled. I admit frankly that it would make life easier for me, but it would be agreeable to you too, I think."

"You're a good man, Edward," said his aunt. "Like your father."

Edward started a little, but laid this remark aside.

"Will you come?"

"Yes."

"Good."

There was a pause. His aunt took up the poker and stirred the blaze.

"How is Leila these days, Edward?"

Edward gave a glowing account of Leila and André.

"It's more than your mother deserved," said his aunt grimly.

"You're wrong there. My mother behaved like a saint to Leila."

"What are you talking about, Edward? It was your father who was the saint in that matter."

"I don't understand you."

"Ah, you don't know that sad old story."

"I know that Leila was an illegitimate child! A by-blow of my father's," cried Edward, all the long-concealed anguish of this knowledge bursting from his throat.

His aunt's face expressed horror. "No, no, Edward! Leila was your mother's child. Don't you see? Your father discovered her betrayal—I daresay she told him, calmly and coldly. She never loved him. She married him for his money. It happened while he was on one of his business trips. Your father was a good man. He forgave her, don't you see? He never told a soul. He sent Claire away to Switzerland, and you and Annie away to Southstone, so there should be no scandal. She came back with the child, everything seemed in order. He adopted Leila, brought her up as his own child, he wanted there to be no scandal. He was terribly sorry for Leila. It was not the child's fault, after all. Claire hated the child from the moment she knew she was pregnant with her. She could cause such a disaster, you see. Ted Milner was too rich to lose. But Ted loved his wife, you see. He forgave her. He never told a soul."

Edward took the poker, which his aunt was waving wildly as she poured out these disjointed sentences, from her hand and laid it down.

"Then how can you know all this, Aunt Audrey?" he said sternly.

"My dear, the child was Gerald's," said his aunt.

It was a foolish, useless, sentimental thing to do, Edward did not doubt. But all the same, before he left Hudley the following morning he sought out his father's grave, and taking off his hat, stood there for several moments in respectful, loving silence.

OUT TO TEA

1903

M I L L I E K A Y W A S a guileless child. If she had lived a
little later, she might have been described as "just out of the
egg"; but at the beginning of this century she was merely
regarded as a sweet little girl, very satisfying in the child
image of the day.

The Kays were a happy family. There was Mr Kay, who
worked at something in an office in the Hudley Town Hall.
Millie did not know what, but he seemed content and had
a friend there, Mr Boyd, who worked with him. (Over him?
Perhaps.) There was Mrs Kay, a loving wife and mother.
There was Millie's older brother, Roy. Millie adored him,
and followed him in all he did. He was at times rather
domineering, at times even rather *cross*, but these bouts of
temper were soon over, and it was clear he loved Millie as
much as she loved him, and only scolded her when she
seemed likely to be straying into danger.

The Kays were a popular young couple, and at times
entertained some guests. Not too many, for that would be
excessive and extravagant. But there were the Royds, who
had a little girl, Lydia, conveniently just the same age as
Millie; there were others from the Town Hall, there were
some from the tennis club. Mr Kay's glory was his proficiency
at tennis; he played for the club and often won tournaments.
It was understood in the family that Mrs Kay had once
shone at tennis too; that was in the past, but its passing

seemed not to trouble her; she still understood everything about tennis and listened enthralled to her husband's description of his games.

A newcomer to the Kay circle was Captain Lermont. He was a soldier stationed with his regiment at the local barracks. He was young and handsome, very fair, with a moustache, and kind to a little girl, and Millie liked him. Yes, she liked him very much. He wound the spring of her mechanical cat and set it going; he swung Millie on his shoulder, he "jumped" her over pools, he laughed with her, he mended Queenie's arm (Queenie was Millie's most beloved doll) when it came out of the shoulder socket; he did not laugh when Millie cried, but sympathised. Millie liked him. Mr Kay also liked him, largely, perhaps, because he played tennis so well. They made an excellent pair, they entered tournaments together and won; they played matches together and won. But Captain Lermont was not at all conceited or difficult. Millie could not, of course, have described how his behaviour on the courts impressed her, but she knew without thinking that he regarded Mr Kay as an elder brother whose advice he respected, and enjoyed being mothered by Mrs Kay. Millie did not even know at first that Captain Lermont was a soldier, but when one day she ran down the garden path to welcome Roy coming home from school, and told him enthusiastically that father and Mr Lermont were measuring the paved backyard to see if they could squeeze a tennis court out of it, he rebuked her sternly :

"*Captain* Lermont."

"Why?"

"He's a soldier. That's his rank."

"He doesn't wear a soldier's uniform," objected Millie.

"He's off duty now for the day."

"Oh, I see."

She did not see, of course, but accepted a senior's dictum, as children do.

Millie having now reached the age of discretion, was sent to a small private school founded by some friends of Mrs Kay. The school, a private house, stood only a few hundred yards away from Roy's Grammar School, so he was able to drop her there in the mornings, and he or Mrs Kay picked her up at noon. Millie went to school joyously, and was happy there. It was fun to have other children to play with. Lydia Royd was there. Millie had known Lydia and all the Royds, all her life; Mr Royd was, it gradually made itself known to her, in a sense Mr Kay's boss. Everyone knew that Lydia's mother was a beauty; very blonde with large blue eyes and slender waist. Lydia was like her, with the same long rippling blonde hair; her eyes were grey, but thick golden lashes accentuated their size. Lydia led and Millie followed.

A new girl now appeared. Her name was Dot Green, which Lydia (and so Millie) thought not very pretty. And Dot herself was (thought Lydia) not very pretty either. She was rather plump, with short thick dark curls and a round, rosy face. She smiled a good deal, and sometimes even laughed aloud.

It turned out that Dot was clever. Her sums were always right, her handwriting was clear and firm, she always knew the answers to the teacher's questions. Now Lydia, unfortunately, was not very clever. She couldn't help that, of course, reflected Millie, but she didn't even try to learn, and would even dash her pencil angily across the page when the answer wouldn't come out. There was no help from Lydia, obviously. Dot, on the other hand, would often break off her own work to explain to Millie exactly what the arithmetic book meant. The strange thing was that Millie always understood her explanations.

"Dot really *is* clever," said Millie to Lydia in a tone of admiration.

"With a name like that you have to be something," sneered Lydia.

"I expect her name is Dorothy really," suggested Millie mildly.

Lydia gaxed at her with contempt.

"Of course if you like her best," she said.

"Oh, I don't, I don't," disclaimed Millie hastily.

A few days later, however, it seemed vaguely to occur to her that perhaps she did. She broached the matter to her mother.

"Can I ask Dot Green to tea?" she said.

Mrs Kay hesitated. She was a good and nice woman, rather less narrow-minded than some, and she found it impossible to explain to such a young child that in politics, religion, income, class and indeed almost everything else, Mr Green and Mr Kay were poles apart. She temporised, and mentioned the matter to her husband.

"I really don't like to—" she concluded.

"Leave it a while, leave it a while," urged Mr Kay. "See what happens. Friendships are too rare to break."

"You're so wonderful, James," said his wife, admiring.

Days went on, Mrs Kay said nothing. Nobody at school asked anybody to tea. It was disappointing. Lydia became more and more capricious and exacting, though sometimes delightful and amusing. Dot maintained a lower level, but was much more cheerful as a companion. Then one morning Millie made up her mind and summoned up her courage. (After all, one cannot play any game well without some nerve, some dash, and Millie was Mr Kay's daughter.) In break-time she walked up to Dot and said quite firmly:

"Can I come to tea at your house?"

Dot coloured and looked surprised, but replied:

"Of course. I'll ask Mother."

At noon Millie ran gleefully to Mrs Kay.

"Dot Green has asked me to go to tea this afternoon," she said.

Mrs Kay sighed and looked at her husband. "I have another invitation for you—I'd rather you were going—" she began. A glance from Mr Kay stopped her. "Well, perhaps —in view of what you said, James—"

"Let her go to Dot's," said Mr Kay sharply, shaking out his newspaper.

"Do you know where Dot lives?"

"Oh yes. It's not far from school."

Accordingly shortly after lunch Millie set off gleefullly to go to the Greens'. It was a beautiful summer's day; the sky was high and blue, the leaves shiny and green; Millie wore a clean dress and clean socks, and her hair, though not either blonde or dark in an exciting way, was smooth, well brushed. The year being what it was, Millie wore a hat, a round straw curving up all round, with a broad black ribbon round the crown, and a narrow elastic to hold the hat on, under her chin. This elastic was apt to become very much knotted in order to cope with the perpetual pressure of the West Riding wind, but as it chanced, Mrs Kay had stitched in a new elastic the night before, and Millie was proud of this.

She took all the right turnings and arrived rather early at the highly respectable terrace where the Greens lived. She trotted joyously up the garden path and rang the bell on the front door.

There was no reply.

She rang again. And again. And again. With polite pauses between.

Her heart, which had sunk very low, rose with a bound when it occurred to her that bells sometimes went out of order!

She knocked.

There was no reply.

She knocked harder.

No reply.

Now in spite of herself tears began to fill her eyes. The corners of her mouth turned down.

Setting her lips firmly, she stood on tiptoe and banged on the knocker with no thought of politeness, but only an overmastering need.

Suddenly the door of the next house in the terrace bounced open, and a round, plump, greying West Riding housewife stood on the step.

"If it's the Greens you want, they're out, love," said she, advancing to the hedge with this pronouncement.

"Out?"

"That's right. They've gone to their chapel bazaar."

"Out?" repeated Millie, utterly dismayed.

There was a pause.

"I was expecting to come to tea here," she explained then, giving herself—how like Millie— completely away.

"I expect there was a muddle over the date, love," said the housewife soothingly.

"Oh, no. No. No. I don't think so."

"You can come and have tea with me if you've a mind, lovey," said the housewife, distressed by the anguish on Millie's face, which seemed to reveal an incapacity to take care of herself.

"Oh, no. No, thank you," cried Millie, terrified. "Thank you very much," she cried again, rushing away down the path. In her headlong flight she knocked off a geranium head, but this misdemeanour, regarded at home as almost a crime (by Roy particularly), made then almost no impact on her mind.

"Well, go home then, love," cried the housewife urgently over the hedge, standing on tiptoe. "Your mother'll be worried if you don't go straight home."

But this was exactly what Millie had decided not to do.

She longed with all her heart for the safety, the security, of home, but was ashamed to go there. What would Mother say? What would Father? What, oh what, would Roy? To be rejected by the Greens was more than she could bear. They had thrown her out, really. Suppose she took a long way home, so long that she did not reach home till nearly six o'clock? After Roy was home from school? Yes, that would be best, decided Millie, her young heart in such pain that her whole body seemed as if torn apart. She turned aside by the church, but oh dear, the clock still proclaimed an early hour. She slowed her pace, but this unfortunately seemed to bring tears nearer. She gulped and swallowed and walked on very slowly and stiffly.

And then—oh what joy—an avenue of safety opened before her. She was passing a rather high wall, somebody's garden wall; of course, reflected Millie, it was the Royds'; and there swinging above the wall, looking delightfully charming, as usual, her beautiful hair swaying in the breeze, was Lydia.

"Hullo!" cried Lydia cheerfully, vanishing as the arc of the swing took her below the top of the wall. She reappeared in the opposite direction. "Hullo, Millie!"

"Can I come to tea with you, Lydia?" shouted Millie.

"Yes, of course. Go round by the gate," commanded Lydia.

What relief! What joy! What gratitude! Millie ran round the corner, found the big metal gates she knew, for she had entered by them before, pushed one diffidently, entered what seemed like Paradise, closed the gate carefully behind her, and ran round the back of the house towards the swing.

"How beautiful you look on the swing, Lydia!" she exclaimed, watching adoringly. "Your hair is very gold, isn't it."

Lydia laughed, but even Millie could see that she was pleased. She continued to swing.

"Could I have a turn now, Lydia?" pleaded Millie at length.

"Well. Yes. I suppose so," said Lydia.

She brought the swing skilfully to a standstill, and dismounted. "You get on—I'll give you a push."

Joyously Millie mounted. It was not quite as easy as it looked when Lydia did it, but after some wriggling back and forth of her sturdy little buttocks, she managed to seat herself.

"Now I'll give you a push. But you must help yourself by pushing with your feet," ordered Lydia rather crossly.

Millie tried hard to obey. But somehow she failed. Her legs crossed each other, the swing's ropes became entwined, the home-made contrivance came to a sudden halt.

"You are *silly*," said Lydia with scorn. "You're not doing it properly. And you're too heavy to push. Look—I'll go and fetch—" she broke off, ran round the corner of the house and disappeared.

Millie, much cast down, waited a few minutes for her to reappear, then as she remained out of sight the little girl slipped off the swing seat and diffidently followed. To her joy she found a nice smooth piece of grass at the side of the house, with a tea-table set and in use, Lydia squatting on the grass eating a sandwich, and Mrs Royd and Captain Lermont sitting in deck chairs. Millie smiled with pleasure and went and stood by Captain Lermont's knee. He smiled and patted her shoulder.

"Oh, Mummy," said Lydia, carelessly waving the sandwich in Millie's direction : "Here's Millie Kay come to tea."

"Good," said Mrs Royd. Millie felt better, because Mrs Royd said this as though she meant it. "Lydia, fetch another cup, dear."

Lydia, having stuffed the rest of the sandwich into her mouth rather rudely, Millie thought, rolled up off the grass and went towards the front door of the house.

"I hope you don't mind me coming to tea, Mrs Royd,"

said Millie anxiously. She wondered whether to explain about the Greens, but hesitated, thinking it might be unmannerly.

"Not at all, dear," replied Mrs Royd. Her voice was kind, and, of course, she really was very beautiful. "We're very glad to have you, aren't we, Jack?"

"Very," said Captain Lermont, smiling and stroking Millie's hair. He was such a kind man, reflected Millie, *very* kind, and of course handsome.

Lydia returned with a cup and saucer for Millie, and they all ate a very good tea. Millie thought that Lydia and herself went on eating perhaps rather longer than was polite; Mrs Royd's invitations to more cake became rather forced, and Captain Lermont glanced once or twice at his watch.

"Now suppose you two children go off and play with your ball," said Mrs Royd at length.

"I don't want to play with a ball," said Lydia crossly.

"Go and swing, then."

"Millie doesn't know how to swing, and she's too fat to push."

"I'm not *fat*, am I?" pleaded Millie, distressed.

"No of course not. I'll come with you and give you a start," offered Captain Lermont. "Come along."

He offered a hand to Millie to pull her up from the grass, and with Lydia bouncing along on the other side of him they went to the swing.

"No—*this* is how you get on, Millie," explained Captain Lermont. "*This* is how you run to get up some speed. Let Millie have a proper turn, Lydia."

When he explained, somehow it was all easy, and soon Millie was flying through the air, laughing happily. Never a selfish child, she presently—sooner than she wished, but one must not be selfish—brought herself to earth for Lydia's turn. Lydia, however, was not there, and Captain Lermont was not there either. Millie paused. It seemed to her that she vaguely heard voices round the back of the house in the direction of the gates. Mr Royd might perhaps be coming home now, she reflected, and Lydia might have gone to meet him. Millie was not terribly fond of Mr Royd. He was quite all right, of course, and Mr Kay made no complaint of him; but to tell the truth, he was rather *plain*. Short and plump and dark, not very well shaved, Mrs Kay hinted, and though kind in general, sometimes a little snappy. Need she go to meet him? Perhaps just a couple more turns on the swing? Why not? She climbed carefully back on the swing, took the ropes in her hands, ran as she had been taught by Captain Lermont, and was soon joyously in the air.

She now perceived what she had not noticed before; that there were windows on this side of the house, windows belonging to rooms, evidently. Yes—there was a room on the ground floor, a kind of morning-room where probably the Royds ate their breakfast. There was a little pointed window on the top floor, an attic where the Royds' maid slept, probably, reflected Millie wisely. (Where was she today, Millie wondered? And answered herself; her afternoon off, I expect.) There was a rather large window on the first floor, no doubt a bedroom. At this point Millie screamed, her grip on the swing ropes relaxed, and she fell off. The swing hit her in its descent, but fortunately not on the head.

The reason Millie had thus relaxed her control was that as the swing passed the bedroom, the window was violently flung open and Mrs Royd threw herself halfway out of it. She hung there; her beautiful golden hair matted with blood, her arms dangling. It was obvious that she had no idea what she was doing; she was unconscious. Millie, horrified, gazed beyond Mrs Royd into the bedroom, and there she saw Captain Lermont beating Mr Royd. Yes! He struck him again; the blood spurted; the Captain then seized Mr Royd in his strong brown hands, round the throat. Mr Royd's eyes closed and he fell backwards. It was clear to Millie that Mr Royd had entered the room, that Captain Lermont was already in it with Mrs Royd. Now suddenly Mrs Royd was pulled violently back into the room. Millie screamed and fell off the swing.

When she came to herself again the bedroom window was closed and everything was quiet except that Roy was standing beside her in a fury. His bicycle lay on the grass beside him.

"What do you think *you*'ve been doing?" he shouted at his sister. "You are the end, Millie, you really are. Here Mother told me to call for you at the Greens' on my way home, and I called there and the house was all shut, and the woman next door said a little girl in a straw hat had come to the Greens' for tea and run away, and of course we didn't know where you could be! Anywhere in Hudley! I've been to the Greens' three times! They were upset, of course."

"Did Dot cry?" enquired Lydia with contempt.

"Good heavens, no! She shouted at me, you've never heard the things she called me—"

"You wouldn't like that," said Lydia, pretending sympathy.

"Yes, I did. She was spirited, anyway. Most girls are too soppy. But as for you, Millie—Mother is in fits. Father's gone to the police." In a low grumpy tone, as if ashamed (and indeed he was ashamed of publicly showing affection for a sister) he added: "I've been in fits myself."

"But why did Dot go out when she'd asked me to tea?" wailed Millie.

'She didn't ask you for *today*, you donkey. It was to be arranged in the future. How did you come to be here, anyway?"

"She asked herself to tea," said Lydia. "It was very rude, and you're rude too, Roy Kay, rushing in like this and making me drop a teacup." Indeed the cup and saucer lay broken on the grass nearby.

"All right, I'm very rude. I don't care—I had to find her."

"How did you know she was here?"

"I saw her on the swing. I shouted at the gate but you didn't bother to come."

"I was in the kitchen, fetching a cup and saucer for my father."

Millie groaned.

"Are you all right? Get on the back of my bike," urged Roy, lifting the bicycle to its wheels.

"I don't think I can," said Millie faintly.

"Don't be silly. Mother will be in fits till you're found. Come along."

Ought she to say anything about Captain Lermont? Ought she to leave Lydia to find whatever there was to find in the bedroom upstairs? Whom to ask to come and help Lydia? Millie had not the faintest idea.

"Come along," repeated Roy angrily. (He really was in a fearful temper.) The habit of obedience was too much for Millie, and she took a trembling step towards the bicycle. "Please thank Mrs Royd for her hospitality towards my sister," said Roy, sarcastic as usual.

By clinging tightly to Roy's waist, Millie managed to remain on the step at the back of the bicycle until they reached home. Mrs Kay, bursting into tears, clasped her erring daughter tightly in her arms, sent Roy for the doctor, and began to put Millie to bed. Millie, however, was not satisfied; she showed a disposition to cling to her father's neck and murmur something—but what?—in his ear.

"What is the matter, Millie?" asked Mr Kay, perplexed by his daughter's anguished expression. "We are not angry with you—it was not your fault—it was not anybody's fault," he added hastily, glancing at a stern bearded gentleman standing by who proved to be Dot Green's father. "It was nobody's fault," he repeated.

"Thank God she is found," said Mr Green.

Millie, rather surprised by the introduction of the Almighty into the conversation, not habitual in the Kay household, nevertheless thought Mr Green was rather nice—not a cross man, she thought, and she took courage to whisper to her father :

"Do go to the Royds', father."

"Why, dear ?"

"Do go, Lydia will be alone."

Mr Kay and Mr Green exchanged a glance.

"I don't see why," began Mr Kay.

There was a pause.

"There are rumours," said Mr Green in a low reserved tone.

"Do go !"

"Will you accompany me, Green ?"

"I will."

It was not till the next morning—for the doctor had given Millie a sleeping pill—that Mr and Mrs Kay came into her bedroom accompanied by a tall severe-looking elderly man, dressed in navy blue with silver trimmings. A uniform, Millie thought. Could he be a policeman ? Millie thought he could. Mrs Kay seemed flustered, flushed and nervous, and propped her daughter up on pillows with a trembling hand.

Mr Kay looked very serious.

"Tell us everything you did yesterday afternoon, Millie," said Mr Kay.

Millie obeyed. It was painful to detail the Green episode, but Roy's suggestion that Dot had intended, not a rejection for that afternoon, but the promise of a future arrangement, was soothing, and the damaged geranium lent a suitable air of apology to Millie's account. Then she had passed the Royds' wall, then she had seen Lydia swinging, then she had asked if she could come to tea, then Lydia cheerfully agreed, then she went into the Royds' garden, then she had had tea with Mrs Royd and Lydia and Captain Lermont—Mrs Kay started—then Captain Lermont had most kindly shown Millie how to manage the swing, then she had swung by herself, then Lydia and Captain Lermont had gone away, then Millie had stupidly fallen off the swing, then there was Roy—she came home with him.

"Ask your questions, Inspector," said Mr Kay, grave.

"When you were swinging, Millie, did you see through the windows of the bedroom on the first floor?"

"I believe I did," faltered Millie with a false air of brightness.

"Were two men there?" pressed the Inspector.

"Perhaps."

"Who were they?" Millie was silent. "Did you know who they were?"

"Was Mr Royd one of them?" suggested Mr Kay.

"Sir," objected the Inspector, but Millie said cheerfully: "Yes."

"Who was the other?"

Millie was silent, gazing from one to the other of her interlocutors in alarm.

"Oh Millie!" burst out Mrs Kay suddenly, weeping loudly: "Poor Mr Royd and Mrs Royd are both *dead*. The other man must have murdered them!"

"Oh, no!" objected Millie. "He would never murder Mrs Royd. Mr Royd killed her, and then he killed Mr Royd. That would be the way of it."

"Who was this man, Millie?" urged Mr Kay. "Millie, if you recognised him, you must say."

But Millie was silent. Never, never would she reveal dear Captain Lermont's identity. Get him in trouble? Never. But to resist her father was difficult. And then suddenly she thought she saw—dear Millie—how she could manage concealment.

"He wasn't in uniform," she said.

WATER, WATER

1910

I n t h e W e s t Riding cf Yorkshire the problem of water
has always been a talking point because it is a matter of
serious and continued concern in men's minds. Every part of
the inhabited world needs water for human and animal
consumption; the West Riding needs it for industry as well.
Cloth cannot be made without water to wash the sheep's
fleece and later unite the woven fibre into a continuous
fabric; presently it was discovered that tumbling water could
also be a useful source of power. Now the West Riding,
containing as it does a millstone-grit part of the Pennine
Chain, is full of tumbling water; hundreds of small streams
hurl noisily down the rocky slopes—the very language, in-
cluding words like becks, delphs, cloughs, bottoms, mosses
and so on, reveals what a watery vocabulary is necessary to
describe the teeming landscape. It is well known to economic
historians that it was tumbling water which took the textile
trade from flat East Anglia, where you had to put up a wind-
mill to get any power, to the West Riding. (The East Anglian
sheep were finer, but the water barely oozed.) That the
human, cattle and textile uses of water are here sometimes at
variance, and water rights a dear possession, is obvious and
local history, full of argument on the matter down the
centuries, shows it all too well.

The rural district of Moordale, comprising the slope of a
steep rough hillside, occasionally interspersed by small

pastures, was edged on the south by a mere beck but on its northern boundary by a stream which, though swift and shallow was almost broad enough to be called a river, the Eddle. The hillside teemed with water. The neighbouring town of Duckersfield had previously concluded an arrangement with Moordale to take some Moordale water and pipe it away to their populous city. They paid a fee, built their own reservoir and seamed the land with catchment trenches, which was all very well until there came a dry summer.

The Moordale Rural District Council, in the early years of the twentieth century, were in session.

"Why should we build bridges across the Eddle all of a sudden? We never had 'em afore," said Councillor Crabtree peevishly.

Councillor Ormerod, in the chair at the monthly meeting, felt vexed. He longed to reply sharply: "I am aware of that, Councillor Crabtree." But to say that was as good as to tell that cheap incomer shopkeeper Councillor Crabtree feller that the Ormerod family had inhabited Eddle Hall for some three centuries, and that was the sort of thing Charles did not do. Besides, he reminded himself sardonically, everybody present knew the fact, even that new schoolmaster chap, Frank Hollis. He therefore restrained his temper and replied with his usual calm: "A request has come from the Haighland Council, which we are bound in courtesy to consider."

"Let 'em build their own bridges."

"The river Eddle is half in Moordale, half in Haighland," put in the clerk, in the tone of an official who knows he is supported by documents.

"In that case they should pay half."

"I believe Haighland R.D.C. are ready to consider this."

"Well, why need we have *iron* bridges? Wood would cost less."

"Iron would last longer."

"Nay! Only if they were painted every two year," put in Councillor Firth. Large, burly, slow, he was a farmer, and had a small bridge or two on his own land.

"An iron bridge in such a beautiful valley as Moordale Dene is an insult to the environment," threw in Frank Hollis with contempt.

"Oh, we all know you think of nowt but beauty," said Crabtree disagreeably.

"That's not true, Councillor!" cried Hollis, his temper and colour rising.

"Now, Frank," said Councillor Greenwood soothingly. Youngish, with a couple of children at the National School, he was a great friend of the schoolmaster, and his friendly tone had some effect. "Can't you take a joke?"

"May I ask, Mr Chairman," began Councillor Lumb (owner of a mill down the dale, almost in the little town of Moorfoot), "whether these proposed bridges are to be for vehicles, or merely pedestrians?"

"Vehicles!" exclaimed Crabtree in horror. "You'll be wanting 'em of stone next."

"If we are to have bridges, it might be as well to build them properly while we are about it, rather than take two bites at a cherry as it were."

"No doubt they would be very convenient for *you* at *your* mill," sneered Crabtree.

"Councillor Crabtree, I resent that imputation," said Lumb hotly. "In any case it is totally untrue. Most of my workpeople live in Moordale and don't need to cross any river; those from Haighland cross the big stone bridge in Moorfoot. Our wagons take the main road down to Hudley, or up across the Pennines into Lancashire."

Several councillors looked severely at Crabtree, who saw he had gone too far. He looked down, snorted crossly and managed to get out in a surly tone: "No offence intended."

Lumb could be seen struggling but eventually murmured without conviction: "In that case, none taken."

"Have we made any enquiries about (a) the location of the bridges (b) their probable cost?" enquired Greenwood.

"Location, yes. Haighland have made suggestions," said the clerk, naming them.

"Have you a comment, Councillor Firth? You probably know the terrain better than any of us."

"Well, yes; those are sensible," Firth said, nodding. "They're all at the foot of our lanes."

"As to price," began Crabtree, glad to regain his dominance.

"May I propose from the Chair," broke in Ormerod hurriedly: "that we ask Mr Walsh, our clerk of council, to obtain estimates for wood and iron bridges? Of various breadths," he added.

"How will he do that?" queried Crabtree.

"Advertise in Hudley and Annotsfield newspapers," answered the clerk.

"Why not Bradford as well?"

"Greater distance means extra transport and extra transport would mean extra money."

"Well, I'm glad you're beginning to see some sense," said Crabtree. "I'll second that proposition."

"A proposition from the Chair doesn't need seconding," snapped the clerk, who was tired of Mr Crabtree.

"Those in favour? Ah, that's unanimous," said Ormerod, relieved. "Well now that that minor matter is disposed of for the moment, let us turn to our major problem: the water supply."

Everyone sighed, recognising the magnitude of the affair.

"Have there been any further developments, Mr Walsh?"

"Yes, Mr Chairman, I'm afraid there have. At our last meeting we mentioned the streams below the Edge, you know. I wrote to the Duckersfield Corporation, and received their reply this morning. I am afraid," he continued, visibly swelling with indignation, "that Duckersfield are adopting a thoroughly dog-in-the-manger attitude. They take our water, use it themselves and even sell it to other boroughs! Yes, they do! But they won't give us a drop. They say that ground below the Edge—"

"Full of water," put in Mr Firth.

"—was listed in their Bill before parliament, you know. So it belongs to their water supply. By law."

"How can that be?"

"It's one of their catchment areas," groaned the clerk.

"Well, it's fairly ridiculous, I think," said Mr Firth slowly: "that here's Moordale, bursting with water all over—"

"Aye, it's one of the biggest catchment areas in the Riding. The land, you see, slopes our way."

"—every dip in the ground is full of water, and water falls over every rock, and yet we who live here have to fetch it in jugs and bowls, like."

"And the children at school here have to walk a quarter of a mile to get a drop," burst out Frank Hollis, crimsoning.

"Surely not, Mr Hollis," said Ormerod. "There is a trough, holding a good supply of water, by the gate I understand—"

"The National School water-supply has been condemned by the Medical Officer of Health in Hudley."

"Do we come under Hudley? It's a good many miles away."

"Only eight. Yes, as regards the Medical Officer we do. It was an arrangement . . ." began the clerk, rueful.

"If we were reported to the School Board, they'd close the school."

"Never!"

"Aye, they would! It's no use you saying Never! Mr Crabtree. A condemned water supply is dangerous. Typhoid. The children are in danger every hour."

"Forbid them to drink the trough water."

"I do, of course. I've covered the trough and put up posters and forbidden them to drink from the trough. Miss Sykes and I do all we can. But you know what children are. The children," shouted Frank Hollis, beating the desk in front of him with his fist, "are in danger every hour."

"We all know you care for the children, Frank," said Greenwood apologetically.

"Then do something about it, for God's sake."

Everyone was shocked by this open reference to the deity.

"Yes. We must no longer hesitate," said Ormerod. "I had not realised how sharp was the necessity."

"I think we'd better leave it over the summer, and see how we get on," said Crabtree.

"Nay! We left it last summer and we were all short."

"You haven't children, Crabtree," said Firth. "I have three. Greenwood here has two, and Parker who isn't here tonight has one. He lost the first one."

There was an awful pause, and even Crabtree dared not ask how Councillor Parker had lost his eldest son.

"Mr Lumb has children—well, his daughter Margaret's out of school by now, but there's another—and Mr Ormerod has grandchildren. Of course they don't attend the National School here. They go away, like."

"That makes our responsibility the greater," said Lumb quickly.

"The responsibility of this Council to the children of Moordale is total," said Ormerod.

"I understand," resumed Lumb, firmly business-like, "that Mr Walsh was to approach Lord Mountlace's agent—Lord Mountlace owns all this land—" he explained to forestall an objection from Mr Crabtree, "about possible services."

"Yes. I approached Mr Ward, as instructed," said the clerk. "He felt that the spring near Box Farm was too small and too near the farm for our purpose; to use it for the whole area would deprive Box of water for the cattle."

"How do you manage for the mill, Lumb?" said Ormerod.

"I draw from lower down the dale, where the two rivers have united."

"You will want to be in on this scheme, then?" Mr Crabtree as usual.

"Of course. Equally of course, I shall pay Moordale R.D.C. for the water the mill consumes."

"How is our finance, Mr Walsh?"

"Excellent. We don't owe a penny and we have no loans outstanding; in fact we have a credit balance. If we implement a water scheme with reasonable economy I don't think we need put much on the rates."

"Ah, the rates!" exclaimed Crabtree in tones of anguish. "There will be a row about the rates."

"There will be a row about the children," said Frank Hollis in a dangerous tone.

"Mr Chairman," began Greenwood—he was always so moderate and practical that everyone was willing to listen to him: "May I suggest that we obtain estimates, and further advice from Mr Ward, and then hold another meeting, a special meeting for Water Supply?"

"*More* delay," snapped Frank Hollis.

"I support Mr Greenwood. We need full information before we can take a sensible decision," said Lumb.

"And then we must call a meeting of our ratepayers," put in Mr Crabtree in a tone of triumph.

All the members groaned.

"A very sensible suggestion, Mr Crabtree," said Ormerod coldly.

"His lordship's agent should be present at any such meeting, I think," put in the clerk.

"And a waterworks engineer," added Lumb.

"And the Medical Officer of Health," snapped the schoolmaster.

"Tickets must be sent to ratepayers, and ratepayers alone," insisted Crabtree.

"I don't altogether agree," said Frank Hollis in a hurry. "Surely everyone who lives in Moordale—"

"It's the ratepayers' money we shall be spending," said Lumb.

"Money, money!" grumbled Hollis in a low tone.

Crabtree turned angrily on him. "If you gave more thought to money, Mr Hollis," he began hotly : "I believe—"

"Well, I think that is all we can usefully do on this question tonight," said Ormerod firmly. "I declare the meeting closed."

The meeting broke up. The chairman and clerk settled down to discuss the wording of the advertisements.

"I'll walk with you a little way if I may, Tom," said Lumb to Greenwood.

Greenwood, half sorry to miss the chance of a talk with Frank Hollis which might serve to calm him, half glad to miss a duty he rather dreaded—he knew Frank's temper well and had listened to his angry complaints about the way the world was run often before—of course assented, for Mr Lumb was in fact his boss, Greenwood being the highly respected foreman of the Lumb mill.

"The back door's the nearest for us both," said Lumb, and they went out together that way.

"How do you think this water business will be dealt with, Tom?" said Lumb.

"We shall need a lot of trenches cut hither and yon across the hillsides, just below the brows, like," said Greenwood. "To catch the water as it flows. Leastways, that's what Duckersfield has."

Lumb would like to have exclaimed : "Damn Duckersfield!" but considering their relative positions he thought it would be unbecoming, so he merely said : "And then, pipes, I suppose."

"Aye, pipes. That's where the money'll go," said Greenwood mournfully.

Meanwhile Frank Hollis, having had a violent confronta-
tion with Mr Crabtree in the front hall, had slammed out
into the bare little playground. Mr Crabtree waddled ahead.
It was drizzling slightly. Firth, smiling with real amusement
—his farm had a spring—was at his side.

"*Water, water everywhere,*" said Frank.

"Well, we need it," said Firth.

They came to the gate.

"I'll just catch Crabtree and butter him up a bit," said
Firth.

"You do that," said Frank, laughing.

"Well, you ruffled him, you know," said Firth, walking off.
They parted.

Under the lamp at the gate stood a girl. Everyone in Moordale knew who everyone else was, even if they were not on
speaking terms. Hollis therefore at once recognised Lumb's
older daughter, Margaret. He noted before that she was
rather a pretty girl, with wavy fair hair and blue eyes, not
too plump, and tallish. He raised his hat—everyone wore
a hat or cap in those days—and murmured with cold
politeness: "Miss Lumb". He had taken a couple of strides
away when he remembered, turned and strode back to her.

"Oh, Miss Lumb," he said apologetically: "I'm sorry, excuse me, but your father has left, you know. He went out by
the other gate with Tom Greenwood."

"Oh," said Margaret, rather taken aback. "Well. Thank
you. I've been to Hudley for my First Aid class and come
back on the Moorfoot tram. I just thought I might as well
call for him. It doesn't matter."

She looked at him with some interest, for she found his
voice attractive and his manner courteous. He was tall, very
tall, too tall, she observed, so tall and so thin that he seemed

to bend over in the middle; his face was pale and haggard, his forehead high; his eyes were large and brown even seen through the hideous steel-rimmed spectacles then in vogue. She also noticed that the navy blue suit he wore was ill-cut —probably "off the peg"—and shabby, thin at the elbows and in any case of poor cloth. She herself was also wearing a navy blue suit—"costume" was the word then—but the cloth had come from her father's mill and been cut by a good tailor.

"Shall you be all right alone? It's very dark under the trees in the Dene," suggested Hollis, his strong protective instinct overcoming his shyness.

"Oh, yes. Moordale's my home, you know, after all," said Margaret, smiling. But at this moment the rain, hitherto slight, decided to pour down heavily. The wind abruptly blew a strong gust round the corner. Huge heavy drops plopped into the water of the trough by the gate. Good heavens, she would get wet, she would get soaked, reflected Hollis in anguish; it was a good mile and a half to Moordale Lodge from here and though there would be shelter under the trees in the Dene the rest of the road lay open to the moorland. What could he do? Ah, of course!

"My deputy head, Miss Sykes," he began, breathless, "always keeps an umbrella here—this building is my school, you know—"

"I know," agreed Margaret.

"—if you could wait a minute, just a minute, I could fetch it. Rather shabby, no doubt, but still an umbrella—after all."

"Thank you. That would be most kind. I'll just shelter by the wall."

"Yes, yes, by the wall," agreed Hollis, overjoyed. "I'll run."

He suited the action to the word, and was back in a very short time carrying a brown umbrella with a long handle.

"It's what they call an en-tout-cas, really, I believe," he

said, getting the umbrella up after one or two efforts. "A sort of parasol, you know. You observe the pink flowery border. Very dashing. Made to use both in sun and rain."

"I hope Miss Sykes won't mind," began Margaret.

"Oh, she'll be delighted," said Frank with enthusiasm. "Miss Sykes is a very good person—truly good, you know. She taught in Moordale for many years. She hoped to be principal here, I'm sure, and was saddened when I was appointed, but she has been so good to me, so helpful and loyal. A truly good person. Splendid with the children, especially the difficult ones. I shall be back at school to-morrow morning before she arrives, you know, and the umbrella will be with me. So no harm done."

"But you'll tell her you borrowed it?"

"Of course."

Margaret now perceived that there was a slit in the silk of the old en-tout-cas, and this slit was allowing the rain to descend on her neat navy cap and her face. Shall I tell him? No! He would be hurt, and she would not hurt him. Why not? She just would not.

At this moment Frank Hollis, whose eyes, because of his height, were several inches above the top of the en-tout-cas, perceived the slit and the rain dripping through the opening. With a neat, delicate twirl he turned the umbrella round so that the slit halted on his side. The rain fell through on to the arm with which he held the umbrella. He did not, of course, say a word about this adjustment to Margaret. He just felt happy to spare her thus, and his brown eyes beamed.

At this moment Margaret laid a hand on the umbrella to lift it, and looked up. The glances of Margaret and Frank met. Without a word or even a smile they both knew at once the good, kind, honest motives which actuated them both. They were motives of goodwill—warm, true-hearted, affectionate goodwill towards humanity in general. Such motives are not easily found. But when found they are to be

113

cherished. Thus at that moment, over a slit in a shabby old parasol, Margaret and Frank fell in love. Hopelessly, irretrievably in love. In love for always.

It was Easter Monday and the usual "treat" was in operation. For once the weather was fine, and the big field by the Eddle, the only piece of flat land in Moordale, as people liked to joke, was crowded with children, racing, jumping, playing, above all laughing and shouting. Frank Hollis was starting a group for the sack-race, a pistol in his hand (lent to him for the purpose by Mr Ward, Lord Mountlace's agent); the elderly Miss Sykes was assisting parents to stuff their offsprings' limbs into the necessary sacks, Tom Greenwood was supervising a jumping competition; Mr Firth was coping with some perplexed brown and white dairy cows in a corner, where Mr Ward was helping (supposedly) a friend of his who had come to judge them. Lord Mountlace, lean and grey-haired, in good tweeds, was rather disappointed in these cows, for he had lands on which he lived, in a softer southern county, which produced, he thought, finer cattle; he was edging away towards the sack-race, for he had grandchildren and enjoyed the tinies' giggles. Margaret Lumb was helping the Hon. Edith Mountlace to give out an orange to every child. These oranges were piled in clothes baskets, and Margaret would have enjoyed giving out the beautiful golden globes if she had been less afraid of Miss Mountlace, who was old, odd, hunched, rather frowning and witchlike, and unsuitably clad in a huge black cape and short laced boots. Miss Mountlace was just as afraid of Margaret—"this young generation"—as Margaret was of her, so their mutual smiles were rather stiff. They were agreed, however, that the provision of oranges was inadequate.

"We need some more, dear. Two dozen at least."

"Yes, indeed. Mr Hollis!" cried Margaret, waving towards the site of the sack-race, which had just finished.

Frank came running up. His pace was eager, and Miss Mountlace of course saw the whole thing at once. Margaret however blushed and could not manage to speak.

"We need at least thirty more oranges, Mr Hollis. Can you see that they are brought to us?"

"Of course. There are plenty in the pavilion." He ran off.

"Oh, is that a pavilion?" said Miss Mountlace, eyeing the small shed with interest.

"It's a cricket pavilion."

"And who is Mr Hollis, dear?"

"He's the head schoolmaster at the National School in Moordale. It's up the hill where we're all going to have tea."

"I see," returned Miss Mountlace rather gravely. "A nice young man."

The arrival of the oranges prevented the need for further speech.

Hollis, however, finding himself near to Lord Mountlace looking unoccupied, nerved himself and approached him.

"Could I have a word with you, sir?"

"Of course."

"About the water supply."

"Ah. That's a vexed question. I'm afraid Duckersfield are not behaving quite as one could wish."

"It seems rather a shame," blurted Hollis, "that here in Moordale with the land beneath one's feet bursting with water, we should have no regular water supply and have to fetch it in jugs."

"Most of the farms have their own spring, I believe," said Lord Mountlace, irritated by this excessive expression. "Jugs are surely an exaggeration?"

"It's the children," cried Hollis at full blast. "The children in the National School. The water in the trough there is contaminated."

"By what?"

"I don't know. Privies higher up the hill, I expect."

"Moordale is all hills and dales."

"The trough water has been condemned. The children are in danger!"

"Oh, well jumped, my boy, well jumped. I was very fond of jumping when I was a lad. Well, Ward?"

"I think we are to move off towards tea now."

"Good. By the way, Ward, what is all this fuss about the water supply? I thought you saw the Council about it long ago?"

"The Council can't make up its own mind, that's the trouble."

"Well, get it fixed."

"Where is Margaret?" said Mr Lumb crossly two months later. He always came back cross from the meetings of the Moordale R.D.C. nowadays.

"It's her evening for her First Aid class," replied his wife. "She's not back yet."

"Why is she always off to classes and such?" said Mr Lumb. "It's unnatural. A girl like her—pretty and all that—should be playing tennis and going to dances."

"Margaret has always been rather serious," said Mrs Lumb.

"I don't like it. Let's send her off to her aunt in London for a bit—some of the bright lights, you know, might do her good."

"Margaret is not very fond of your sister, unfortunately," said Mrs Lumb carefully.

"I'm aware of it. I'm not very fond of her myself. But Moordale's too small for Margaret. Get Lizzie to invite her."

There was a pause.

"Why are you so worried about Margaret all of a sudden?" said Margaret's mother, shrewdly.

"Well—never mind. I shouldn't like her to marry the wrong sort of man."

"She shows no inclination towards any young man at present."

"Ah. Well. We may think so. Pity that young Ormerod went off and married someone else."

"She never showed any interest in him."

"She never tried," said Lumb irritably.

"You can't fall in love by trying, Philip," said his wife. "Or out of it either. I tried hard not to fall in love with you, a textile manufacturer like everybody else, but I couldn't manage it."

"Well, that's the trouble," said Lumb, frowning, then smiling all the same. "There's a young man on the Council—damned insulting young whippersnapper—"

"Not that gaunt schoolteacher she was talking to at the Treat?" cried Mrs Lumb in alarm.

"That very same. Prejudiced, impertinent, argumentative, conceited—he talks as if he were God."

"Would it be a good idea for you to have a word with her? About how rude he is to you, I mean?" said Mrs Lumb, foreseeing endless family discord if the schoolteacher approached the household.

"No."

"She's very fond of you," said Mrs Lumb, heroically suppressing jealousy—sons turn to mothers, daughters to fathers; it's only fair, she thought.

"That's why. I want her to stay so."

"She often says she really wants to be a nurse," ventured Mrs Lumb.

"Nonsense," said Mr Lumb brutally. "Why should she go in for such a hard life? She's pretty and domesticated—she should marry."

Mrs Lumb felt disheartened. In spite of Margaret's

preference for her father, she knew her daughter's determined spirit much better than he did.

"Philip—I think I'll get her off to Switzerland. That school where the Ormerod girl went, you know."

"Well, it might be a good idea," said Mr Lumb with reluctance. "Because it's all very well, First Aid classes and that, Alison, but the last tram from Hudley got into Moorfoot half an hour ago, so where is she now? I think she often meets him."

In fact, his suspicions were justified. Frank Hollis and Margaret Lumb were walking arm in arm together through the rain from the Moorfoot tram terminus to Moordale Lodge, pausing at times to admire the occasional stars. They were very happy. After two or three meetings filled with hope, doubt, discouragement, despair and joy, they were beginning to feel confidence in each other's love.

It was clear, from the crowd of people jostling amiably about the room, that the meeting would be well attended. Frank Hollis made his way towards Mr Lumb. He felt nervous and shy, but had made up his mind that he would accost Margaret's father tonight, whatever distress it caused him.

"Good evening, Mr Lumb," he said.

"Good evening," said Lumb shortly. He was in a very bad mood and hardly able to speak with decent civility.

"I wondered if perhaps Mrs Lumb and your daughter, your elder daughter, would be attending tonight."

"No." Lumb turned to the young man a face quite ravaged by pain. "My daughter left for Switzerland this morning," he said. "She has gone to school there for three years."

"Three years!" exclaimed Hollis. It was a blow under which he reeled. Mr Lumb, he noticed, looked as badly as he himself felt. He turned away, almost staggering in his pain. In fact, he was right. Mr Lumb had seen his daughter off at the station that morning, and at the very last moment she had said to him hardly :

"I shall never forgive you for this, Daddy."

"What do you mean?"

"Just what I say. I don't want to go. You know it and you make me go. I shall never forgive you."

"You will be home for the holidays in a month or two."

Mrs Lumb wept, and her husband spoke with vexation to her.

"I mean what I say."

Mr Ormerod now took the chair. It had been suggested that the Councillors should sit on the platform grouped around him, but Mr Ormerod had been unusually disagreeable about this. It was difficult enough, he had said to himself, to control a meeting when the people quarrelling were in front of you and down on the floor; but if they were seated on each side of you it was impossible. Wagging your head from side to side looked too foolish, and in any case if they began to shout at the same moment—and this was precisely what Messrs Crabtree and Hollis would do, he knew it—one could only look in one direction at a time. So seated on the platform was Mr Ormerod, flanked by the Clerk to the Council, Mr Ward and the Waterworks Engineer from Duckersfield. The Medical Officer of Health was not present, but had sent a letter in his place which condemned the Moordale National School Water Supply in terms so short, cold and clear that there was really no arguing against them. Or so at least Frank Hollis thought.

Mr Ormerod arose and made a pleasant warm-hearted speech of welcome.

"I am sorry not to see more ladies present," said he, smiling at the three farmers' widows, who were present because they indubitably paid the rates.

"You only sent one ticket!" shouted a voice from the rear of the room at this.

Everybody laughed, and Mr Ormerod, accepting the rebuke, smiled and continued: "For it is upon them, I think, and I am sure you will agree, that the burden of an inadequate water supply chiefly falls."

Several men exclaimed: "True! That's right!" and everyone felt comfortably convinced of their own wisdom, in perceiving this.

Mr Ormerod read the Medical Officer of Health's letter. It was so blunt, and scolded Moordale so severely for its long delay in providing a proper service, that everyone looked glum and fell silent. Mr Ormerod judged this a good moment to introduce Mr Ward, who had brought a large local map with him. A good deal of fuss supervened while Frank Hollis fixed this across a blackboard easel and provided Mr Ward with a pointer. Mr Ward, however, knew his employer's lands extremely well, and if his southern accent made rather heavy work of some of the Moordale names, he knew the gradients to a foot, and showed an acquaintance with the heather, cotton grass, bogs and rough bent grass of the area which called forth several corroborating cries of "That's right!" from his experienced hearers.

Mr Ormerod was pleased, and introduced the Waterworks Engineer. Few things are less interesting, however, than a stream of statistics presented orally. At first pleased to learn how much water each individual Moordaler consumed a day, the audience presently grew bored, yawned, even talked to their neighbours a little. Figures of mains and gallons were difficult to visualise, and cubic capacity even more so. When, however, they learned that the new proposals would bring in thirty thousand gallons each day and that the necessary reservoir need not be large or expensively constructed, they relaxed into approval and applauded the Waterworks Engineer quite heartily.

"And now for the finance," commenced Mr Ormerod.

Mr Crabtree gave a loud and deep groan. Everybody heard it and was alarmed. Would the expense be so awful?

"Mr Chairman, I have said before and I say it again, that we ought not to rush into this heavy expense without due consideration."

"We've been considering for four years, Councillor Crabtree."

"Mr Chairman, may I speak?"

"Yes, Councillor Hollis, but please be brief."

"Mr Chairman, we have all heard the letter of the Medical Officer of Health, in which he condemns utterly and totally the water supply to this school. Every moment the water trough remains in the yard here, Moordale children are in danger."

"Pipe the water in the trough away somewhere, then," said Crabtree.

"Where shall we pipe it to?"

"Nay, that's your look-out. I don't care."

"Murderer!" shouted Hollis.

"I won't stay here to be insulted," cried Crabtree, clumsily rising.

"Councillor Hollis, you must withdraw your epithet," said Ormerod firmly.

"I don't feel at all inclined to."

"That is my ruling, as chairman of this meeting," said Ormerod. "Withdraw."

"Shut up and sit down, Hollis," said Lumb, exasperated.

"It's all very well," cried Hollis, "but none of you have children at the school. Lord Mountlace doesn't live here; Councillor Crabtree has no children anyway; Councillor Lumb gets all the water his mill needs from lower down the Eddle. None of you know anything about the children and none of you care."

"Could we possibly have an account of the probable expenses?" put in Greenwood in a calming tone.

"Certainly."

Crabtree and Hollis, both wanting to hear this, resumed their seats.

The clerk detailed the finance required, concluding by saying that in the present stage of Moordale accounts, only an additional twopence would be required on each rate as paid at present.

"Twopence in the pound," enlarged Crabtree.

"Twopence in the pound, of course," said Mr Walsh irritably.

"I've heard it would be six and fourpence on every pound," said one of the farmer's wives with gloom.

"I am glad to be able to tell you that that is incorrect, madam," said Ormerod.

"Let us murder a few children rather than pay six and fourpence, certainly," threw out Hollis.

"Really, Councillor Hollis, do please modify your expressions," urged Ormerod.

"Aye, but, Mr Chairman," said a man rising from the back row : "Could it be true what he says, like? Mr Hollis, I mean. If a child drank summat from trough here, would it be dangerous, like?"

"It might be," said Ormerod carefully.

"Well, then, I think as how we ought to have a piped service properly, like."

"Hear, hear," came from several parts of the hall.

"All nonsense," threw out Crabtree.

"Murderer," said Hollis in a quiet but very distinct tone.

Crimsoning, Crabtree shouted : "I will not stay here to be insulted by a young whippersnapper."

He rose and swiftly, in his ungainly sideways fashion, tripped from the room.

Everyone paused a moment, dismayed. Then Hollis suddenly sprang up and followed.

"After him, Tom!" cried Lumb, hauling himself up from a rather small chair. Greenwood, astonished, obeyed.

Whether Mr Lumb thought that one of the quarrelling men would attack the other, and if so which, it is impossible to tell, and probably Lumb himself did not know his own mind in the matter. But by the time Lumb and Greenwood tracked down the quarrellers in the spring dusk, Crabtree had fallen sideways into the much-discussed trough, and Hollis was either pulling him out or pushing him in. Greenwood thought the former, Lumb suspected the latter. There was a good deal of splashing and slipping in which Crabtree's short but plump and heavy body was—except for his head, which protruded oddly—deeply imbedded in the trough; Hollis actually climbed in, stooped over his enemy and with some expenditure of muscle pushed him up and out, while the new-comers hauled on his legs. All four men were pretty well soaked when Crabtree at last stood on his own feet at the trough's side, supported under the arms by Lumb and Greenwood.

"I thank you, gentlemen," said Crabtree with his usual pomposity. "I was inspecting the tank when my foot slipped." He put a hand to the top of his spine. "The trough should be covered. I understood Mr Hollis to say at an earlier meeting that the trough was covered."

His tone was peevish and accusing as usual.

"The heavy spring rains have swollen the water till it threw off the covering board," explained Hollis, drying his face with his handkerchief. "The paving stones around the base are green with moss and slippery. I'm not surprised you lost your footing."

"Are you hurt?" asked Lumb impatiently.

"Bruised, I fear," replied Crabtree with dignity.

"You have to thank Mr Hollis for saving you from drowning."

Crabtree snorted angrily and offered no thanks.

"You'd best walk home quickly or you'll catch a bad cold," urged Greenwood.

"Take my coat," said Hollis drily.

Crabtree snorted again but did not refuse the coat thrown over his shoulders. Without more words he turned and walked away through the gate.

"That was foolish of you, young man," said Lumb.

Hollis shrugged and walked off.

Yes, the whole affair was foolish. Indeed, silly. And all because people lose their tempers and say more than they mean. Silly, yes. But tragic too. For Hollis died of it, you know. Yes. Typhoid. He'd swallowed some of the trough water. They put up a plaque to him on the school wall, inscribed: *In Memory of Francis Hollis, first headmaster of this school and a devoted member of Moordale Rural District Council.* Of course the plaque vanished with the old school building and wall when the new school—very fine at the time, quite inadequate now—was built.

"Frank. Oh, Frank," mourned Tom Greenwood. "Best man I knew."

"He was a nice lad," mused Mr Ormerod, who unveiled the plaque. "Over-enthusiastic, you know. An extremist. Damaged his own cause. But honest."

"Foolish," said Mr Lumb, shaking his head. "Pity."

Mr Crabtree was not present at the ceremony.

The Moordale water supply was a great success. Margaret is an excellent nurse—appointed matron this year in some large southern hospital. She does not often come home.

"ONE OF OUR HEROES"

1848–1974

ONE DAY SEVERAL years ago—it was about 1956, I think—I was sitting on a March evening reading the *Hudley Star*, our little town's evening newspaper, when I encountered this paragraph.

> *A prominent local Esperantist, Mr Joe Dean, of 13, Pickles Street, Hollow Bridge, died, in Hudley General Hospital during the weekend. For nearly half a century he had corresponded with people in over 50 countries in different parts of the world. Among people from whom he had letters were a Tibetan priest, a Paris wine merchant and a Czech miner. Mr Dean had been a textile worker. He leaves a widow.*

I smiled, in fact I actually chuckled, to myself. I looked up Pickles (originally Pighills) Street in my local "Where Is It" directory, and found that it was even more remote than I had thought. Hollow Bridge—I don't know when it got its name; some time in Queen Elizabeth's prosperous days, I expect—was a small, active, commercial suburb of Hudley, down in the valley with an old packhorse bridge across the Hollow and quite a sizeable nineteenth-century bridge leading to a main road over the Pennines into Lancashire farther on. But Pickles Street was not in Hollow Bridge but on Hollow Bank, a steep hilly tract running up the side of the Pennines, with a farm and a weaver's cottage or two here and there

125

scattered about the rough grassy slopes, but really very far away from anywhere. The thought of dear Mr Joe Dean corresponding with people in Tibet, Paris and Czechoslovakia, toiling away at night in Esperanto by the light of a lamp, his good wife knitting at his side, both very proud of his linguistic skill, pleased me. What a race we are in the West Riding, I thought with pride. So obstinate, so individual, with these odd quirks we're so proud of; it may be pigeons, the Messiah, politics, teetotalism or Esperanto, but whatever it is we do it with our might and defy anybody to be amused.

Unfortunately, however—and how unfortunate it was I later discovered all too well—I did not pursue Hollow and Mr Dean further at that time. I was in the middle of another novel and held myself sternly on its track, resisting all Esperanto blandishments.

Time went on and life changed.

I should now explain that there was a man of Hudley, dead before I was born, who was a great benefactor of the town. I will call him Q, because that has nothing to do with his name. Everything about Q, I felt, was just as it should be. His family had lived, landowners, on a high bleak Pennine outside Hudley for some five hundred years—yes, in 1346 there are records. They stonefaced their big timber house in the reign of the first Elizabeth; but even before that they were Constables of the village, honourable, courteous, trusted men; priests occasionally founding University scholarships. A rather touching story, well documented, is told of them in the fifteenth century about a love affair: a young man of the family fell in love with a girl (poor) who proved to be his cousin and therefore within the proscribed relationships for marriage. He fought this up and down with the authorities, in Hudley, York and eventually in Rome; won a dispensation, married the girl and lived happily ever after. I have told the tale elsewhere, and I feel that all the Q's resembled this 1434 Q; a man honourable, faithful, capable of devotion.

Then suddenly the Q's were landowners no longer. In the seventeenth century they suddenly sell their houses, and we find them down in a well-watered valley becoming cloth-makers. Why? One might easily devise a reason. The Q's were Cavaliers, perhaps, in the Civil War, and had to pay such a huge Composition, as it was called, to Cromwell's men, that landlordism was no longer possible, and they had to work. But unfortunately for the historian, the date is not right. The Q's sold in 1666, that is after Charles II was restored to the throne, and Cavaliers were comfortable again. Of course one could invent a gambling father. I tried this and began a story on these lines, but I could not convincingly create a Q who was a gambler, and tore it up.

Why did I trouble myself, at various different dates in my life, with the Q family? Because, quite simply, I have for many years regarded myself as a novelist of the West Riding, and I felt I could not honestly do so unless I included the nineteenth century Q. The Q's prospered tremendously as clothiers, yes, quite tremendously; each generation moved lower down the valley, built a larger mill, acquired a vaster turnover, so that when our Q's father died he left his sons a million pounds, honestly acquired through making fine cloth. But our Q, you see, when he died, having bought out his brother from the family mill, owned only just over £1,000 in the world.

What had he done with all that money?

Well, he built a couple of churches, very fine in the taste of the day; he built rows of solid houses for his workers; he gave a park; he founded a canteen where his workers could buy a cup of tea for a penny-ha'penny; he started a Sunday school, he started education classes for the workers' children; he started a free library; one Sunday stranded in London with nothing to do, he attended St Paul's, heard the Rev. Charles Kingsley speak on the need for thrift in the working class, was so impressed that on his return he called together some rich friends and started a special kind of bank, where you could deposit one penny if that was all you had to spare. (This is still a very solid and prosperous affair.) He became a Member of Parliament for a neighbouring town.

You already see, I am sure, why Q absolutely must go into a novel of mine. I agree warmly. But you see, Q lived the white flower of a blameless life. Nothing is more difficult than to put on paper the story of a good man—because there is no *story* in it. A love affair, perhaps? Well, no; Q married a most sweet, gentle, ladylike girl from a good East Riding family. Her charming, mild face looks down from the wall of the solid well-planned house Q built for himself on a hillside above Hudley. (In the West Riding we are apt to think of East Riding families as rather soft, genteel people.)

Q was a man of taste and good manners. He rode well and kept good carriage horses, their harness and the trimmings of his vehicles done in modest silver. He sat on committees, subscribed to charities.

His life has been written most scrupulously and conscientiously by various members of the Hudley Historical Society. (We have a great many amateur societies in Hudley, you know; well organised and well run, with president, secretary, treasurer, committee, minutes and resolutions and amendments and everything handsome about them.) Yes; Q is well documented. But where is his *story*? And why should it continually trouble me?

Let me just add one detail.

The people of Yorkshire, though warm-hearted, stubborn and loyal to a degree, are not apt to be gracious or forthcoming in gratitude. (During the reign of Queen Elizabeth I, in 1588, James Ryder in his *Commendations of Yorkshire* wrote of the Hudley people thus:

"after the rude and arrogant manner of their wild country, they surpass the rest in wealth and wisdom."

In the twentieth century—I write in 1974—this is still a good portrait of them, so I don't suppose they were very different in the 1880's.) When, therefore, I record that these people gave enough of their own pennies to build a massive statue to Q—the plinth alone stands ten feet high—and that 15,000 persons attended his funeral, you will understand that Hudley really appreciated him, and that he must be celebrated in a story.

From time to time, therefore, I made very sincere efforts to delve more deeply into Q and really probe him to his depths. Whenever I paused between novels, my thoughts turned to Q. And one day it happened.

I looked up everything about the Q family in the local reference department of our Municipal Library. I had read it all before, of course; but to re-read was my duty, and should be done. I noticed three rather interesting points about Q's life.

The first was that in 1847 Q and his brother withdrew from Hudley for a couple of years. They went to live in a less industrialised part of Yorkshire, establishing themselves in a pleasant country estate. Of course it was in a way all quite natural. There had been a big row throughout the nation about a Parliament Bill dealing with religious education in schools. Some people thought the Church of England unduly favoured above those of Nonconformist belief in the Bill, others thought the reverse. The row was very real and bitter. Indeed Q's father, presiding at a public meeting where the matter was being discussed with the usual West Riding bluntness, was so upset by the vehemence of the quarrel that he quietly fell forward, dead. This was enough to anger the Q brothers against the West Riding, of course. Or was it? At any rate, they shook the dust of Hudley off their feet for a few years and settled down elsewhere. What were they doing in those years? Anything? Probably nothing. They were far too decent and well-behaved to be suspected of any disreputable act. Still, I noticed the absence. It was said they came back full of plans for the good of their work-people. Interesting.

Then I observed that when Q returned to active West Riding life and became a Member of Parliament for the neighbouring town of Annotsfield, in 1857 Palmerston invited him to second the Commons' Address of thanks on the Queen's speech at the opening of the session. Of course this is a familiar gambit for encouraging new young members, giving them a start, getting them up on their feet, bringing them to the notice of the House under favourable circumstances, and so on. Very pleasant and agreeable for the young member concerned. But one wonders a little—or at least I did—why Palmerston showed this favour to Q.

To understand at all why the great Lord Palmerston was hated by some Englishmen, adored by others, consecutively and even sometimes simultaneously throughout his political life, it is necessary to plunge a little into what was happening in Europe at this time. It was the period when Northern Italy was trying to throw off the Austrian yoke, and Hungary, alleged by Imperial Austria to be a vital part of the Austrian empire, was alleged by many Hungarians, led by Kossuth, to be by ancient treaty an independent republic, merely allied to Austria.

It seemed clear to some people that Palmerston approved of these attempts at freedom. Indeed he was all too often in trouble on this score with Queen Victoria, who, being connected by kinship with several courts and not liking rebellious subjects much in any case, took a different view. One has only to read the Queen's letters—and of course I read them—to see how sharply and often she rapped him over the knuckles for sending off despatches unfavourable to Austrian and other Powers without submitting them first to his Sovereign, how bitterly she complained of his various phrases too favourable to insurgents. When scolded, this able but difficult man remarked cheerfully that he regarded the sight of any people struggling for liberation from a foreign yoke as a happy event in which all well-wishers to mankind should rejoice. Queen Victoria replied crossly that she was not to be regarded as someone who was not a well-wisher to mankind, but really Viscount Palmerston's behaviour was quite out of line. (I am sure Albert found it shocking; speaking procedurally, he was right.)

And yet England did nothing to help the insurgents openly.

In point of fact Palmerston was in a very difficult situation. Austria's European duty, as he saw it, was to provide a barricade against the encroachments of Czarist Russia. He therefore did not wish to weaken Austria too severely. Neither did he want France to take the opportunity of revolts in Italy to pop down and install herself there. It was awkward. But he managed it on the whole well—these complex situations suited him; he had all the courage necessary and was always ready to plough through them, if the worst came to the worst, with a gunboat. That he sympathised, as a true-born Englishman, with struggling Italians and Hungarians, while deprecating their weakening of a central power, is perhaps a fairly accurate statement of the case. What Q had to do with all this however seems—

But what, what, what is this? What about that third interesting point? Did I not read also that in later life, twenty years or so after Kossuth's rebellion, Mrs Q opened a bazaar in Hudley on behalf of her husband, who was absent, travelling in south-eastern Europe? What was Q doing down in the Balkans, travelling alone? Why? Nostalgia? Could it possibly be that Q approved of Kossuth? Surely not. Never let it be said. It *was* said, and with a good deal of emphasis, that Kossuth had sent a letter to Palmerston by an Englishman. Could it be? Well, hardly. But of course that would explain why this tall, fair, quiet, rich manufacturer with a genteel wife and tasteful silver harness was agreeable to the dominating, autocratic Palmerston.

At this point there vaguely floated across my mind a remembrance of Mr Joe Dean, who had corresponded, it was said, with a Czech miner. What was a Czech miner in those days, for heaven's sake? I must see Mr Dean. But he was dead. When did he die? I hadn't the faintest idea. Then find out, I exhorted myself. Then since his address then might give some clue as to his recent whereabouts I went to the local Registrar's and secured Mr Dean's death certificate, took the death certificate to the *Hudley Star* and looked him up in the paper. Yes, there he was, address 13 Pickles Street, Hollow Bridge, 1956.

"There's another cutting about that chap somewhere," said a young man who sat with an immense pile of cuttings before him. "I'm sorting these, you know, ready to throw some out. Rather interesting, I remember thinking. Here you are."

"Thanks."

It is not in the West Riding nature to exclaim "Eureka!" shrilly. So I merely gave a subdued exclamation and sank into a chair. I was flabbergasted all the same. For the cutting read, in the newspaper dated April 7, 1952

Was it coincidence? asks Mr J. Dean, of Pickles Street, Hollow Bank, in a reference to the fact that last week's local page, with its references to Q, appeared in an issue which also recorded the death of Mr K. John Czernowski? Mr Dean goes on to explain the link as follows: "How many Hudley people realise the greatness and fame of Q in the history of Hungarian independence? It was in 1906 that a Hungarian boy-Esperantist (now Professor Bakonyi of Budapest University) asked me to correspond with him from Hudley as he wished to have information about the General Q who played such a major part in the Louis

Kossuth liberation of Hungary. I was glad to help him with information, and pictures, but the greatest point of success was when I wrote and told him that my Esperanto pal, John Czernowski, was the son of the personal aide to Q.

When Q returned to Hudley, he brought his Hungarian protégés with him. John, the Esperantist, the son of one, became a part-time fire-brigade man. Through the medium of Esperanto, Mr Czernowski was able to play, and beat, famous European chess champions.

Needless to say, I wrote that day joyously to Joe Dean's widow. She was still alive, asked someone to telephone me, and a few days later received me at the house she still inhabited in Pickles Street.

Pickles Street is very agreeable when you reach it. A neat terrace tucked along the side of an otherwise very sparsely occupied hill, gazing without interruption across the valley where the little river and the canal run side by side. But the access to the terrace is uncomfortable, at any rate in a car. First one ascends a Pennine hill, then turns sharply down the slope. The lane is steep, narrow, occasionally grassy and always stony, with unexpected corners. The house was small but neat and well cared for, approached by three large flat stone steps and a little iron gate. Mrs Dean was very much a Yorkshirewoman, large, bosomy, active, very honest, very forthright, a little impatient with me and my errand, which she thought not much of, but quite ready as always to accept her duty towards her husband's fame—clearly she thought Esperanto "silly work", but Joe had always been like that and for his sake she put up with it. She brought out all the papers which remained to her.

But here I came upon a bitter disappointment. Absolutely nothing remained except an English-Esperanto dictionary. I pressed Mrs Dean about the boy Bakonyi, later a professor.

Yes, she thought she had heard of him. Yes, come to think
of it, she had heard of him. Joe had attended a conference
when Bakonyi was there—she thought. Had she heard of
Q? Well, yes; everyone had heard of Q. About his fighting
with Kossuth in Hungary? Well, no. About his bringing
back two Hungarians with him to Hudley? Well, Mrs Dean
thought they were Poles. There were two, she believed; but
did Q *bring* them? They appeared in Hudley about that
time, she thought. The son of one of them, Czernowski, was
Joe's great friend; an Esperantist, you see. Son or grandson,
she was not quite sure. That two Poles or Hungarians suddenly appeared in Hudley about the time of Kossuth's defeat
was certain. Their names, so different from our own Yorkshire, and therefore the constant play of friendly jokes,
actually figured above shop windows. I had myself, as a
child, seen these names in Hudley there. This in itself meant
capital; to start a shop needed money. Why should these two
strangers come to a smallish West Riding textile town unless
somebody brought them, encouraged them, lent them
money? Well, if it was anybody it wasn't Joe, of course, said
Mrs Dean firmly. Joe was foreman mechanic down at—
she pointed to a large textile mill in the valley; it was con-
venient-like for him, you see, he just popped down a path
through the fields and came out at their door. But as to
having money to set somebody up in a shop, of course that
was out of the question. Her son knew no more, she was
sure, and anyway he was in Canada; her daughter Harriet,
though it was true she was always her father's favourite and
might have heard more about Bakonyi, had unfortunately
died in childbirth in London, some years ago. Her husband
had remarried, said Mrs Dean grimly, sensible, of course,
with a girl child to bring up, but all the same one never
liked it. Would I have a cup of tea? I accepted, and as we
drank together pressed again about Bakonyi.

"I never took much notice of it all, like," said Mrs Dean, grimly practical.

Please, gentle reader, please, PLEASE, if you have in your possession any papers of historical interest, KEEP THEM. Give them to your local municipal library in a strong envelope or sizeable folder, or lay them in a chest or give them to your solicitor; but keep them.

Thwarted in Pickles Street, I began to write letters. I wrote to our Hudley Member of Parliament, who advised me to write to the Hungarian Embassy in London. I wrote to this Hungarian Embassy, dropping names etc. suitably. They advised me to write to a Hungarian cultural society, who advised me to write to another. This in charming language asked for the first name of Professor Bakonyi, since the name of Bakonyi in Hungary was as frequent as Smith in England. Later they told me regretfully that there was no Professor Bakonyi on the staff in Buda Pesth, and later still, that the records of Kossuth's army had all been burnt in the last war. I was told of, and tried, a Hungarian gentleman in England who was preparing records of all Kossuthians who had taken refuge in this country. I learned from him that indeed two likely Poles had come to northern England; one to Liverpool and thence to Hudley, and one to Kidderminster. At this I leaped into the air again, for Kidderminster is a town which weaves carpets; and the great manufacturer who alone was regarded as Q's rival in Hudley was a Carpet man. Indeed, this last man, I discovered, had employed a Garibaldian refugee from Italy, whose skill in design lent much to the Hudley carpet's beauty. It began to occur to me that Hudley, far from being a dull, reactionary, plodding sort of place, really had concealed several of these refugees of European liberty successfully from their enemies. I mentioned this to one of our local historians at an Annual Meeting.

"But, of course," said he. "Don't you know about Admiral Stanton?"

"I'm afraid not."

"But my dear child," said he kindly from the heights of his great age, "it was one of the great jokes of the period—while the police of Europe were scouring the continent for Mazzini—I hope you know about Mazzini?—"

"Of course. The great Italian liberator, precursor of Garibaldi."

"Well, while the police of Europe scoured the continent for Mazzini, Sir James had him tucked safely away in that lonely ancestral old house of theirs, you know, on the top of Hollow Mount."

"Are there documents to corroborate this?"

"Well, no. Not documents. But so-and-so the historian," he went on, naming a rather well-known historical writer, "was once writing a history of the Stanton family—a Stanton ancestor was once Sam Hill's executor—the case of Sam's Will was the origin of the *Bleak House* story—"

"I know, I know. I made a novel of Sam's sad tale."

"Well, this historian asked me to go through the Stanton papers to see if I could find corroboration of the hiding of Mazzini in Hollow. But I could not."

I sighed.

"Of course," said he, "conspirators against the Establishment don't write notes of all their revolutionary doings, to be used against them at their trials, you know."

"Then what gave rise to the story?"

"Admiral Stanton lost his job on account of his friendship with Mazzini. He was in Parliament, you know, a junior Cabinet Minister of sorts. And there was a great row because the Post Office turned up letters addressed by Giuseppe Mazzini to Italian conspirators, one of them was a would-be assassin, in fact, in which Admiral Stanton's name and address figured. Of course, the Admiral knew all the revolutionaries of the time: Cavour, Herzen, Mazzini, Kossuth, Garibaldi, the lot. He couldn't and didn't wish to deny it. He had a business in London, a brewery, I think it was, and often visited it and saw these friends. But it was as if he had corresponded with a Russian Communist during the Cold War period, you know. Imagine what Queen Victoria must have said! The Admiral resigned."

I leaned forward. "Have you," I asked with great earnestness, "ever heard that Q went out to Hungary and fought at Kossuth's side?"

He lowered his voice and looked aside. "Often," he murmured.

"Hurrah!"

"But of course I don't believe it."

"Why not?"

"No evidence for. Evidence against: Kossuth came to England in 1851—he even came to Hudley! He had a tremendous reception. But Q took no part in it. He never attended a single meeting where Kossuth was present."

"But if it was dangerous?"

"Oh, pooh. Q would not have cared about that. He was not in politics; he was a man of wealth and sure position."

"His wife might have cared. And his brother."

"But why do you think the mild well-behaved Q—"

I poured out all my details of Esperanto, Poles, Joe Dean.

"Not a scrap of real evidence, just a lot of talk. The tale is often repeated, of course, but it is regarded as not authentic, and so is not mentioned in official accounts."

"No smoke without fire?"

"Why should Q go and fight in Hungary?"

"Why indeed?" said I. "He may have felt rather cramped, in Hudley."

"I've always thought him noble, of course, but a bit of a bore."

"He inherited a million and died worth a thousand."

"You admire that?"

"It's rather exceptional in Hudley. He travelled in southern Europe twenty years later."

"Did he indeed? I wonder if he took Booth with him?"

"Booth?"

"His groom. He was with him when he died. Very devoted."

I remembered the silver harness. "I wonder if Booth had any knowledgeable descendants?"

"No; I can tell you he hadn't. Poor-law chap; no relatives; unmarried."

"You've researched this Q story yourself," I accused him.

"Possibly, possibly."

"The descendants of those two Poles might know something."

"The descendants of one of them are all dead."

"I shall try the other set."

"Well, have fun!" said the historian, laughing in kindly derision as he waved farewell.

To assume that I, a mere novelist, should succeed in a piece of research where the local historian, so sound, so meticulous, had failed, was graceless, I knew; but all the same. . . .

A name as strange as Czernowski is easy to trace in Hudley, and accordingly I presently found myself spending a very pleasant evening with the present descendant of one of Kossuth's sergeants. There he was, John Czernowski, indubitably the grandson, for he showed me certificates, a lean, handsome man, dark and suitably Polish in looks, lively in mind and tongue. He had a pleasant, good-looking fair-haired wife in her thirties, a fair teenage daughter, pretty and agreeably shy, and a large black and white cat, clearly an indulged favourite, very sleek and glossy. The house, one of a short terrace very high on a Pennine hillside, was spotless, comfortably furnished, well equipped, everything quiet, respectable, prosperous. Best of all—and I could hardly restrain my jubilation when I realised her presence—there was his mother, old, of course, but brisk and upright. Actually the widow of Joe Dean's friend the Esperantist. She spoke of her late husband quite frequently, calling him "Kage".

"That was what they called him," she said firmly. "His name was Kazimir, you know, but they called him Kage. Pronounced it that way, I expect."

She told a nice tale about Kage's father—actually Kossuth's sergeant!—defending another foreign workman (another?) who was receiving less pay from his boss because he could not speak English. "He paints with his hand, sir," said the sergeant, "not his mouth."

(Just the man for a sergeant in a revolutionary army.)

My voice quite trembled, my throat was dry, as I stammered out the question: "Did Kage or his father ever speak of Q?"

"No."

"No? Oh, surely . . ." I cried in an anguish of disappointment.

"No."

"Had you heard of Q?"

"Vaguely."

Seeing my look of horrified discomfiture, she explained:

"Kage and I married late, you know. I was thirty, Kage was well on in his forties. Neither of us had seen anyone we liked, before," said Mrs Czernowski with the candid dignity of truth. "It was 1924. Q was dead long before that."

"Oh, but surely. Your father-in-law must have spoken of Q."

"Never."

"I believe you, of course, but it is hard for me to believe

you," said I, briefly recounting the tale of Q and his Polish protégés.

"It was an old story by then," said the senior Mrs Czernowski firmly.

"People often don't know the early history of their parents," said the junior Mrs Czernowski with intent to soothe. "Well, aristocratic people may, because they're taught it, I expect. But not ordinary people like us."

"Still, it comes out in bits and pieces sometimes," suggested the daughter.

"I never heard anything about Q," said John, thoughtful. "My mother's got a few cuttings, like."

These were shown. The merest formal insertions of deaths and marriages. Not even the fatal Joe Dean–Bakonyi paragraph which had set me on my quest.

"Did you ever hear the name Bakonyi?"

"Never."

"Joe Dean?"

"Yes, I think so. Yes, I know the name. He was one of the Esperanto group. I don't think I ever met him. The group met once a week on Wednesday evenings, at the secretary's house."

"Did your husband ever play chess with men from other countries, by means of Esperanto?"

"Oh, yes, indeed; he was a great chess player. There was always posting of letters to do, with stamps for abroad. Sometimes I copied the letters for him."

"Did he ever play chess with someone in Hungary?"

"I don't remember," said the senior Mrs Czernowski with regret. "I didn't address the envelopes, you see. Foreign addresses are so different from ours, aren't they. Kage understood better how to write them, than I did. But I doubt that he ever wrote to Hungary. You see," she suddenly volunteered, all her life and love in her tone : "Kage wanted to forget all that past sad history. He wanted to be English.

Or perhaps he just wanted me to think so," she added with a wistful smile. "He was especially anxious for our son to be an Englishman, so as to have a better chance than he had himself. And yet to remain a Pole, if you see what I mean. He didn't change his name, like some, anyway," she concluded proudly.

"Well—I thank you warmly for your confidence, and I apologise for taking up your time in vain," said I rising.

"It has been a pleasure to receive you," said John with ceremony. "We deeply regret that we have no information for your service. But we can do no other."

I almost sobbed with grief and disappointment as I drove down that very steep hill, with the lights of Hudley twinkling far below. It was almost worse, perhaps, because the outward unimportant details were all corroborated. Though slightly different from the *Star*'s account: Esperanto, chess, Joe Dean—but alas, no Q.

But suppose there had been corroboration? Suppose Kage had known Q, known him well? I am a novelist, a storyteller, and I could not prevent myself from telling the tale as it might, so easily, have occurred.

Suppose, one night in London, Q had been introduced to Mazzini. A noble figure, worn and thin, with a white beard, high forehead, strong straight nose, piercing black eyes; a man living in a small house above a post office, surrounded by the dogs and cats and birds he loved: a brilliant talker, his slight Italicisms so endearing; teaching (for nothing, of course) small Italian boys the noble history, the noble aspirations, of their race. Idealism poured from his lips, he spoke it freely to the Italian organ-grinders and hawkers of terracotta casts who thronged the streets of London; his accounts of Austrian tyranny were appalling. His friends were the finest people of the day: poets such as Browning, social workers such as Toynbee; English and American travellers of all ranks were proud to convey his secret letters to revolutionary Italians.

One night perhaps he was about to set out for Italy on one of his many secret visits. The Stantons were alarmed at the thought of his doing the dangerous journey alone. Q suddenly offered to take him. What could look more innocent to police than a rich English textile manufacturer with an English attendant valet escorting an elderly grandparent to Rome? Q almost choked with eagerness; all his warmth of heart, his love for his fellow-men, his longing to do something noble for them, perhaps (we do not know this) his fatigue with textiles and Hudley, the huge prosaic mill at home and his ten-year-old and quietly happy but unimpassioned childless marriage, swelled to his throat. His eyes gleamed. Obviously he was as honest and trustworthy as the day. The Stantons took Mazzini, Q and Booth to a London dock, and by night, the tide being suitable, embarked them. The scene itself was thrilling: the dark river flowing and lapping, lights on the banks gleaming, great hulks of ships silently passing; what an adventure! Q hastily wrote a tender note to his wife, protesting business in Paris; the Stantons put it in the post and promised to allay her fears. Q would not be long away, they thought. The ship was bound for Genoa, not for France; dangerous, no doubt; but still . . .

But unfortunately the expedition to Rome was not a success—Mazzini's expeditions were never a success. He had the feeling, the tongue, the words, to rouse; but his temperament was as unsuited to commanding troops as his black velvet waistcoat and frock coat to military action. Q extracted him from one or two awkward situations, then decanted him on a small freight ship sailing for London. The Captain declined to take Q, but would embark Booth if he signed on as a seaman. Booth however declined to leave his master. Q paid the captain substantially, and gave him a note to present to Stanton's brewery in London. What to do now? A hand-

some passenger ship was leaving for Marseilles in a day or
two, but Q could not bring himself to take it. He was enjoying this new, colourful, noisy, exciting world too much.
Without quite knowing why or how, he found himself under-
standing and not blaming Mazzini's failure, but longing for
a fiercer champion. This chap Kossuth, now, fighting the
Austrians in Hungary? All of a sudden he was marching
and riding across northern Italy, then embarking from the
eastern coast at Ancona, crossing the Adriatic (where the
Austrians, not a seagoing nation, had no ships) landing at
Trieste, marching north-east towards Pesth.

If Genoa had been exciting, this new country was in a
frenzy. Portraits of Kossuth, talk of Kossuth, everywhere. In
some villages young men leaving home to join him for
Hungary, while wives and mothers left at home arranged to
send despatches to him without a moment's delay. In other
villages old fellows, still wearing the Austrian uniform they
had worn proudly in the Austrian army, refused food and
shelter to men they thought of as abominable rebels. We do
not know, of course, how Q and Booth reached Kossuth,
and it is beyond my powers to invent their route and its
adventures. But we must remember that Q had money and
was a good horseman, while Booth was an experienced
groom. They knew no Hungarian, which was awkward, but
then also they knew no German, which in the unsettled state
of the country was perhaps a good thing. Kossuth relying
hopefully on Palmerston continued to expect that England
would support Hungary, although no official envoys were
sent; Austria, with official English envoys at her court, could
not believe the old alliance was broken. Thus to be English
was fairly safe from both sides. Many nationalities were
already represented in Kossuth's forces, so two Englishmen
were not noticeable.

I imagine Q and Booth, after hair-raising adventures,
arriving at the massive doors of some baronial Hungarian

establishment, dismounting from admirable if mud-splashed horses, and asking with English calm for Kossuth. They are ushered by guards into the great man's presence. He looks at them enquiringly.

"We are English," says Q with native calm, "come here to fight at your side."

"Why not?" says Kossuth who had studied English in an Austrian prison, courteously: "You are very welcome."

The truth is, I think, that the two men took a fancy to each other. Physically they were rather alike; both being tall, solid and blue-eyed, with broad high foreheads, strong features, thick wavy hair and pleasant smiles. Both were men of absolute integrity; Kossuth, surrounded as he was by generals, who disagreed with him, crossed his plans, failed their rendez-vous and eventually by surrendering betrayed him, may have recognised this trait and welcomed it in Q.

There was no difficulty in providing the two Englishmen with the rough clothes now worn by the rest of the army; big clumsy boots, long rusty spurs, wide white trousers and coarse linen shirt hanging out over them, long white cloak of coarse wool and round felt hat banded by the Hungarian colours, red blue and green. There were plenty about, and swords and pistols, lying with dead Hungarian bodies on the innumerable battlefields. Not that the frequent conflicts were exactly battles; merely skirmishes across the wide Hungarian plains, each force trying to manoeuvre the other into a disadvantage. I do not believe, of course, that Q was ever a "general", rendering great service to the cause of independent Hungary as Bakonyi believes; I think he was probably some sort of aide to Kossuth, or allotted as a member of a group of "honvëds" as the word went, the equivalent of the German *Landstürm*, or as we might say, territorials, galloping hither and thither on his fine horse.

That he galloped enough we may judge from the written memoirs of another similar honvëd, who speaks of being

often in the saddle for twelve hours a day. At night they
bivouacked on the open plain, sleeping close together round
a huge fire if they could find trees for the blaze. Half their
horses were unsaddled, so that some lay down, others slept
on their feet; but the other half always remained in saddle
and bridle, with guards attending them, so that on the
slightest hint of surprise the troop could be on horseback,
ready to attack within three minutes. The honvëds could not
shave, or even often wash; their clothes, like themselves, grew
tattered and dirty. There were nights when they fell in with
gipsies and musicians; then they sang and danced with all
their ferociously gay national abandon, and would have
continued this lively enjoyment till morning if their officers
had not commanded them in the strictest terms to sleep
awhile so as to be fresh for battle next day.

Could we suppose that the lieutenant and sergeant in
command of this group were Pulaski and Czernowski, whom
we met later in Hudley? I think we could. We see mild,
conventional Q and the devoted Booth sitting on the icy
ground, watching with an immense glee, a joyous feeling
of escape and release, the tumultuous dance of these handsome people, their white teeth sparkling, their long black
hair blowing, their fine lean limbs tossing rhythmically in
tune with the wild music.

The high point of Kossuth's campaign was his capture of
Vienna. Hardly a capture, perhaps; he just walked in and
occupied it, nobody making much objection. With other
officers Q was billeted upon a friendly Count; and this
Count had not only a handsome and dignified wife from one
of those provinces in Italy held by Austria, according to
Mazzini against the people's will, but also a beautiful sister,
the Countess Hélène. This young Hélène was really very
beautiful; very young, with glorious dark eyes and masses of
curling dark hair, a delicious sweetness, a tendency to regard
a fair Englishman as a romantic hero, very delightful to a

married manufacturer of thirty-eight. She really seemed to love him. Q was sorely tempted, and perhaps Booth urged him on. But Q was an honourable man and a faithful husband, and he and Hélène parted in anguished tears, with no harm done.

Why Kossuth retreated from Vienna with scarcely a shot fired when part of the Austrian regular army walked in on him we cannot really tell. Enough that he withdrew from the Austrian capital, Q of course with him, and Q resumed the wild and scampering life he had been living before Vienna. By this time, we judge, he had become a reasonably good shot, and quite got over his nervousness with a sword. Q and Booth would be a tough pair to meet on a dark night, and were not too gentle about scragging an enemy sentry if it seemed necessary. By this time Q was an officer, I expect, and no doubt with his English thoroughness a conscientious one, and thus one moonlight night when the distant mountains were covered in snow, after a hard fight during the afternoon he was inspecting the chain of sentry posts set around the group, in company with the devoted Booth. (I wish I knew the appearance of this man : I see him as short, sturdy, pug-faced, dark in complexion with a bit of a scowl, a dimple and thick eyebrows, but of course I do not know; he may have had a florid face and winning smile for all I know. But I don't think so.) All the men at the sentry posts were awake and watchful and Q was returning cheerfully to the bivouac fire when at the foot of a tree in the moonlight he perceived a human body. They advanced and turned the body roughly on to its back. It was a woman dressed in a man's uniform; the long hair which fell over her shoulders betrayed (in those days) her sex. Q stooped and turned up her face. It was Hélène.

The sharp agony of this blow struck Q to the heart. Lifting the girl in his arms, he conveyed her to the fire and strove to revive her. But she was dead, with a bullet through her heart. Some of his men recognised her; they all grieved for her. They thawed by a fire the ground near a tree, and spent much of the night digging a deep grave—a precaution against wolves—with their swords and hand-bills. They then wrapped the poor young beauty in the cleanest blanket they could find, buried her, fired a salute of pistols above her grave—rather dangerous, this, with the enemy so close—and placed upon it a cross made out of twigs from which they peeled the bark. Did Q cut off a lock of her gloriously curling hair and put it in his pocket-book? I think so.

I cannot but feel that from this moment Q's view of the adventure upon which he was engaged, changed radically. Hitherto it had been a glorious joke; now it was a heart-breaking tragedy. He might even have been sickened by the slaughter which battles invariably produce. It might also be, on the contrary, that a hatred welled up in his heart for the men who had killed his love. He was a man of honour, in any case; he had come here to fight for the freedom of Hungary and he intended to fight for the freedom of Hungary. He was devoted to the noble Kossuth.

How Kossuth then lost his war, is a matter so complex it is hardly to be deciphered. The Hungarians of the plains quarrelled with the Magyars of the hills and both quarrelled with the Poles; the generals quarrelled with each other and with Kossuth and showed an invincible tendency to march in the wrong direction. The aristocrats did not support Kossuth; the older villagers remained nostalgically Austrian; the Russian Imperial Army came in. In a word, there were some three battles; one general surrendered; the affair was over, and all that remained for Kossuth and his men was to get out of Austria, to reach safety over the border in Turkey.

It was a long gloomy march. We can easily imagine the sad poetry, the melancholy reflections, that filled the men's souls as they prepared to leave their native land. Home was behind, exile in front: the superb views of forest-clad hills, backed by distant blue Carpathian mountains, the winding silver rivers did not soothe their hearts; the difficulties of the route—sometimes marshy, sometimes pebbly, sometimes smooth steep slippery rock—the harshness of the wind and rain, the scarcity of provisions, by their irritation almost relieved the deeper feelings. For Q, the prospect of finding himself in Turkey, a place regarded in the West Riding as so distant as to be almost fictional, almost non-existent, certainly totally barbaric, must have made him blench; however he kept his English calm, we may be sure, gulped down the native porridge without complaint, shared his scraps of bacon with his comrades, at one time even had the honour of proffering a piece of cheese to Kossuth himself; and marched.

A deep relief when at last the column came to the border and could see safety ahead was followed by the sorrow of departure. To step out of one's homeland into foreign parts, into a place where one is an alien, does not belong, leaving behind all those near and dear, is extremely and deeply painful. Kossuth very wisely gave the men a serious and noble address, not minimising the anguish of parting but holding out the hope, even if distant, of return and stressing the need for good behaviour. They crossed a river, traversed a mile or two of plain, and came to a large army of Turkish troops, who were encamped in rows of neatly lined green tents outside a town. Here a ceremony was performed, always very painful to soldiers; they had to give up their arms. Men and horses were then counted and listed, which gave a painful impression of servitude; they were allotted space for bivouacs, and after a night of rain next morning marched off surrounded by Turkish regulars.

In this, however, reality proved better than their fears; the Turks in their red fez, blue jacket and white trousers proved to be jovial, cheerful masters. Though the arrangements for food were somewhat irregular and slapdash, food was definitely provided. A grief which befell many soldiers was the confiscating of their horses. Many of the men had previously served in Austrian Imperial regiments, and their horses bore the imperial stamp; all these were sent back by the Turks to the Austrian government, which claimed them as their property. Only these horses privately bought could be retained by their owners. Q and Booth no doubt retained theirs, as did Kossuth and some of his generals. Soon Kossuth's army was camped in tents and sheds, with the higher officers accommodated in stone houses. There they remained for some months.

The tedium of such an imprisonment is almost unbearable to active men. There is nothing whatever to do, except take two roll-calls a day, groom one's horse and try to rid oneself of vermin. Kossuth held small meetings every day, at which camp matters were discussed, but there was little to be said about the affairs of their country, in which the Imperial government had now completely resumed power.

One morning Q entering this meeting was struck by the downcast appearance of the officers present. Kossuth's noble brow was lined.

"Is something wrong?" he asked, glancing at each in turn.

A very blank look was his first reply, then he heard mutterings in which the name of England seemed to be grumbled. He turned to Kossuth.

"The Austrian government intends to require the Turks to expel us," said Kossuth. "There is a treaty."

"The treaty contains no such clause," snapped a general.

"True. But if Austria and Russia combine in the demand," began Kossuth.

"The men would be glad to return to their homes?" suggested Q uncertainly.

"They would return to imprisonment and execution," Kossuth corrected him.

"The demand has not yet been made," said a general.

149

"I cannot believe that England will allow this to happen to us," said Kossuth, frowning.

"Once the demand is officially made, the Turks will yield."

"Why?" said Q.

"They are weak, and Russia is strong, and stands on their northern border."

"The demand has not been made officially yet. We learned of it by chance, from a Turkish Bey here who heard it from some court spy."

"Then we must implore Lord Palmerston's aid at once."

Kossuth turned to Q.

"Will you take a letter to him?" (The telegraph was not invented for another fifteen years.)

"Yes," said Q.

This laconic answer revealed the character of the man but not the tumult of emotions which at that moment filled his heart. There was nothing he wanted more, at that moment, after the experiences of the past few months, than to be in England, but he was incapable of deserting Kossuth to please himself by achieving such safety. He therefore added:

"If you think I am the most suitable messenger."

A series of growls from the assembled generals sounded affirmative.

"It will be dangerous," offered Kossuth.

Q shrugged his shoulders.

It is on record that this letter—certainly written and delivered, though whether carried by Q or not we do not know; the name given is not his, but it does not figure anywhere else; after all was Q using his own name?—reached Palmerston within ten days of its leaving the Hungarian camp at Widdin.

One slight glimpse we might have of Q on this journey. When crossing the Channel, the white cliffs of Dover now appearing to him out of the mist, he might—yes, I think he did—at this first sight of England he might have drawn out from his pocket-book the dark curly tress of Hélène, and confided it, with what anguish of heart, what enduring love, to the waves. Yes, I think he did. And so at last he reached London.

We see him climbing the stately Foreign Office steps, telling the doorkeeper firmly that he bore an urgent despatch for the Foreign Secretary, being ushered at length into the elegant room where Palmerston transacted his business. He perceived at once that the great man was a great man; the massive body, the heavy lined face, the steady frown, the large penetrating brown eyes, declared his power plainly enough.

"From Louis Kossuth," said Q, proffering the letter. He stood stiff and straight, though he was tired.

"How did you travel?" enquired Palmerston, opening the letter.

"I slipped through," began Q, hesitating as he remembered all the shifts by land and sea, the horses abandoned, the captains bribed, the couriers deceived, the lack of food, the cold, the seasickness, the escapes from soldiers, magistrates, police, which he and Booth had endured and triumphed over.

"Well, never mind," said Palmerston impatiently, reading the letter.

Q, a man of sense, was at once silent.

"H'm," said Palmerston thoughtfully. "What is it like at Widdin, eh?"

"Vermin and idleness."

"And is this," tapping the paper, "believed?"

"Yes, sir."

"To be imminent?"

"Immediate."

"Well."

"Do you require me to return with a letter to Kossuth, sir?"

"No. I shall send a despatch of the most sternly official kind." He thought of Queen Victoria and gave a grim smile. "You are English. Where do you live?"

"Hudley in the West Riding of Yorkshire."

"Go home and forget this adventure," said Palmerston. "It would never do for Kossuth to be known to be writing direct to me. Unconstitutional."

Which explains, as one may say, everything.

So Q returned to Hudley, to his sweet and gentle wife, to the mill, to fine worsted cloth, to his charitable efforts. To canteen and saving bank, to churches and rows of houses, to educating his workers' children, to railways and mill chimneys. Peaceful, if dull—and peace is so much to be preferred to the dead body of Hélène. Sometimes, I think, Q rode up to the old house in the hills—with Booth, of course. And no doubt they silently compared the bare Pennines and narrow rocky streams to the forested slopes and broad rivers of Hungary, compared the Yorkshire folk who greeted them with slow but friendly words to the frantic music and whirling gipsy dancers of Hungary. But I do not think that Q ever mentioned Kossuth or Hungary again to anybody. He did not forget his adventure, but was too mindful of Palmerston and the exiles to speak of it. Did he find Hélène's grave when he travelled in South Europe in 1876? Difficult, I fear.

About the exiles: Palmerston put his foot down and the Queen, shocked by Russian inhumanity, supported him; the Turks, heartened, politely evaded the Austrian and Russian demands. Some of the exiles turned Mahometan and some others joined them in Turkish employ; some drifted away to other countries—some even as far as England. Not one was ever handed over to their conquerors.

Kossuth toured England and the United States in 1851, where his fine oratory brought him a fine reception. He actually came to Hudley and held meetings there. Did Q contrive to be by chance away during this period? Kossuth most likely had never heard of Hudley. How should he? Q would not trouble him with the name of an obscure small town in a northern county far from London, which in any case was probably as difficult for Hungarians to pronounce as Szegedin is by ourselves. So he made no enquiry for Q? He knew naught of his English honvëds.

Q was presently elected member of Parliament for the neighbouring borough of Annotsfield, and as I have said, was chosen by Palmerston to second the Address of thanks on the Queen's speech. We may now guess why.

After many quiet happy years together Q's wife died, and presently in due course Q, having lost most of his money, mainly by expense on social welfare work but partly by mistaken investments outside England, eventually in a seaside resort far from Hudley died too. Booth was with him when he died.

But whether Q went to Hungary or not to help Kossuth, I do not know. He was certainly one of our great benefactors. Was he one of our heroes too? I do not know. What do you think?

II

Present Occasions

AT THE CROSSING (1971)

ON THE STATION (1971)

IN THE QUEUE (1971)

FOR THE WEDDING (1971)

REMOVAL (1971)

MOTHER-IN-LAW (1974)

AT THE CROSSING

1971

MISS ELLIS, STROLLING slowly uphill in a steepish
street in the West Riding town of Hudley, was halted by a
small poodle trotting in front of her. The poodle, white, very
curly, decidedly pretty but with rather a dispirited air, was
attached by a pale blue leather lead to the hand of a plump
woman walking in the centre of the pavement. Miss Ellis
tried to pass the poodle on the right, but the little dog
swerved at once in that direction. She changed her tactics
and tried to pass the fat woman (as she crossly called her)
on the left, but there was not space on the pavement for
this manoeuvre, and Miss Ellis thought it unwise to plunge
into the roadway, down which—it was a one-way street—
vehicles were rapidly swishing. She tried the right-hand side
again. Somehow the pale blue lead wound itself round her
ankle. The poodle looked up at her with sad reproachful
eyes; the lead jerked its owner's hand, and Mrs Jowett
turned sharply on Miss Ellis.

"I beg your pardon," said Miss Ellis stiffly.

"Not your fault," said Mrs Jowett. This was clearly not
her real thought, for her expression was glum and her tone
angry.

Miss Ellis found this artificial forgiveness insulting.

"I'm so sorry," she repeated, rather more stiffly than
before.

"Lulu!" barked Mrs Jowett. The poodle cowered.

"Poor Lulu," said Miss Ellis. It was now her turn to be insulting and she meant her tone to sound so.

Mrs Jowett jerked the lead, and after a moment of acute discomfort, when Lulu seemed bent in half and her claws scrabbled on Miss Ellis's ankles, the poodle was disentangled.

"A pretty little dog," remarked Miss Ellis coldly while this was in progress.

"She's been a good friend to me, has Lulu."

"Indeed."

The two women glanced sideways at each other. They observed that both were pleasantly and even handsomely dressed. Miss Ellis, who was justifiably proud of her tall and slender figure, inclined to the well-cut and quiet; Mrs Jowett, plumper, went in for fur and colour. Each disliked the other's style, but recognised its propriety. They walked on side by side, not quite knowing how to part without discourtesy, and too angry to allow themselves the pleasure of rudeness.

"You think I was taking up the whole pavement, I expect, wandering from side to side," accused Mrs Jowett.

"Not at all," replied Miss Ellis, making the lie obvious.

"There's too many hills in this town," complained Mrs Jowett, panting—implying that Miss Ellis walked too fast for her.

Miss Ellis looked round at the well-loved Pennines on the lower slopes of which the town was built, and gave a modified agreement.

"Perhaps," she said in her high light tones. "Still, I should not care to live in a flat town."

"*I* should," snapped Mrs Jowett.

"A friend of mine," pursued Miss Ellis, eager to express opposition, "who married and went to live in Cambridge— a very level district, you know—used to say that the moment she got out of the train here, in Hudley, she felt better. Livelier. More alive. The air felt fresher here."

"I'll bet she was young to say that," countered Mrs Jowett crossly.

"She was at the time, yes," agreed Miss Ellis.

Her voice held a note which Mrs Jowett, though she could not name it, recognised. But she was not to be wheedled.

"You've lost her then, have you?" she said, harsh.

"Yes," said Miss Ellis briefly, looking aside. "When her baby was born."

"Well—it happens," said Mrs Jowett, matter-of-fact. "I lost my young sister, you know. Same way. Pity."

"Indeed," agreed Miss Ellis, her tone still flat and chilly.

They arrived at the threshold of the pedestrian crossing, and paused. Cars of every shape, size and hue, buses, vans, motor-bikes, flew by.

"Well, here we are. Not that they'll take much notice of *us*," said Mrs Jowett, sour.

"Oh, I don't know," countered Miss Ellis, vexed. "My brother drives and he's always most scrupulous at crossings."

A very young teenager, with dark flowing hair and flowery short pants, came rushing up and put one toe on the crossing. Amid horrific shrieks of brakes, the cars, almost rearing in their effort to stop, managed to prevent their front wheels from trespass on the crossing. The drivers all scowled, and the scowl spread down the long line of traffic. The teenager skipped blithely and nimbly across to safety. She did not even condescend to smile at the halted cars.

"What do you think of that, eh?" demanded Mrs Jowett.

"It's not easy to stop a car suddenly in a yard and a half," countered Miss Ellis.

The driver of the foremost car now made frantic signs to Mrs Jowett, urging her to cross.

"No, thanks. Not for me. I can't hurry," said Mrs Jowett. "I have to wait till there's a real gap, you see."

"Oh?"

"Yes. Rheumatism. I limp a bit. Don't wait for *me*," urged Mrs Jowett disagreeably.

"I can't hurry either," admitted Miss Ellis.

"Oh? Boots too tight?" said Mrs Jowett sardonically.

Miss Ellis's boots were certainly rather dashing; tall and tight, with black and silvery patterns. She was vexed by this attack on them, but managed to laugh.

"No—as a matter of fact they're rather helpful," she said. "They give support. I sprained one of my ankles twice, that's all."

"A sprain is worse than a fracture, they say," said Mrs Jowett, unctuously gleeful.

"It has proved so in my case."

"You should have some of those what-do-you-call-them injections," reproved Mrs Jowett.

"I've had several," riposted Miss Ellis.

"Or physio-therapy or what is it."

"I've tried that too. The truth is," volunteered Miss Ellis coldly, spurred to defence, "I fell down our cellar steps when I was four years old, and my left hip and ankle have always been a little—"

"Wonky," nodded Mrs Jowett, enjoying this depreciating word.

"Exactly."

"Spine a bit out of true."

"Just so. Still, I haven't done so badly until the last year or two."

"You should wear an anklet," urged Mrs Jowett, reproving as before.

"You're quite right. I have done so from time to time. But it's a bit of a bore, you know."

"All these gadgets are. How'd you come to fall, eh?"

"My mother went down to get some milk for me. She told me to stay at the top—"

"But of course you didn't."

"Luckily I was wearing a thick coat and bonnet of corduroy velvet, and this protected me from serious harm."

"You remember your coat, do you? I'll bet you do."

"It was *blue* corduroy," said Miss Ellis dreamily. "A kind of sea colour, you know."

"I'm surprised your mother didn't send for the doctor."

"Oh, she did. But he couldn't find anything seriously wrong."

"Not *then*," said Mrs Jowett with significance, cleverly implying how long ago was Miss Ellis's youth, before the days of X-rays.

"Just so. Still, I've not done too badly until the last year or two, when these sprains came along, you know. But such a happening in childhood, the result of adventure, disobedience, is apt to curb one's spirit."

"Ha!" snorted Mrs Jowett in disbelief.

"What about your rheumatism?"

"Least said soonest mended," said Mrs Jowett, grim.

"The traffic seems to be calming a little now," said Miss Ellis. "Shall we try it, do you think?"

"Well, we might," said Mrs Jowett doubtfully. "Don't wait for me."

Miss Ellis hesitated. It was against her code of conduct to desert a rheumatic patient on a pedestrian crossing, but she disliked Mrs Jowett too strongly to wish to aid her.

Just then a middle-aged man, rather plump and dirty, not well shaven, in his working clothes, with greying untidy hair, came rushing up to them.

"Can you manage, loves?" he cried.

He seized each by one arm, and without a moment's hesitation urged them both on to the crossing. Lulu, excited, barking shrilly, large ears flapping, sprang joyously after them.

"Now then!" the man cried cheerfully to the oncoming cars, nodding his head.

The drivers nodded back and laughed, drawing up politely. The man whisked the pair across. Giving each of the arms he held a vigorous lift, he assisted Mrs Jowett and Miss Ellis to mount the causeway kerb, then shouting: "Ta ta!" vanished away down a side-street.

The two ladies looked at each other, breathless but smiling.

"Well!" said Mrs Jowett. "Safe this time, choose how."

"I think we should all adopt that as our slogan," said Miss Ellis earnestly.

"How do you mean?"

"*Can you manage, loves?* If we all said *that* to each other, and acted on it, the world would be a happier place," said Miss Ellis, blushing, very serious.

"Well, it certainly was a bit of all right," agreed Mrs Jowett. "I'm going in here," she added in a friendly tone, nodding towards an hotel with one of those circling doors. "To meet my husband, you know."

"Shall I carry Lulu for you?" suggested Miss Ellis. "Those doors might be awkward for her?"

"Well—if you would just lift her up into my arms," agreed Mrs Jowett.

Miss Ellis picked up Lulu, caressed her and put her carefully into Mrs Jowett's embrace. Lulu mildly licked her hand.

"Come in and meet my husband," urged Mrs Jowett.

"Well, thank you. That's very kind of you," replied Miss Ellis, smiling.

The two women walked up the steps of the hotel side by side, smiling and feeling happy.

ON THE STATION

1971

M RS E LLIS AND Mrs Gowland, laden with parcels, made their way up the steps under the big Yorkshire railway station to the far platform. Mrs Gowland grumbled bitterly about the steps.

"How they expect us to climb things like these, every time we come to their shops," she said, "I really don't know."

Mrs Ellis, who had an arthritic hip and disliked the steps quite as much as Mrs Gowland, said nothing till she had reached the platform and regained her breath, when she remarked mildly :

"Bert says it's something to do with the gradient."

Bert was Mrs Ellis's husband and Mrs Gowland's brother.

"He *would*," said Mrs Gowland scornfully.

"He says, to make a slope would be too steep or something."

"Then they should have digged deeper," snarled Mrs Gowland.

"Wouldn't that make it worse, Gladys ?"

"Or used more space."

"They know their own work best, I expect," soothed Mrs Ellis.

"First I've heard of it."

"We aren't late, anyway," said Mrs Ellis, looking round.

Mrs Gowland snorted. (It was she who had been so anxious about catching the train.) "Small help from *them*."

If anything, they were rather early. The side of the platform from which the local diesel train would start was empty, and not many passengers were as yet awaiting it.

"There's room on that seat. Let's sit down," suggested Mrs Ellis.

They moved across to the seat with relief, arranging their parcels round their ankles.

"What that girl Nerissa costs me is nobody's business," grumbled Mrs Gowland, looking down at her purchases stuffed into a brightly coloured carrier. "The tights she goes through!"

Mrs Ellis thought Nerissa rather a high-flown name for Mrs Gowland's daughter, who was black-haired and black-eyed, with red cheeks and a plump bosom, who earned a good wage at a multiple store and was rather apt to be rude to her mother. But she thought Nerissa might not have an easy time with Gladys for a mother, and her father, too, though a friend of Bert's, was often rather grumpy—and no wonder. So she said kindly, defending the girl:

"She's young and pretty, she wants to look nice."

"She needn't split her tights every week."

"Now, come, Gladys, it isn't *every* week," objected Mrs Ellis mildly.

"Well, I don't like her going out with holes in her tights," explained Mrs Gowland, virtuous and solemn. "It might give people ideas, holes in her tights."

"People?"

"Boys," said Mrs Gowland, ominous.

"Ideas?"

"Well, you know what I mean. Or perhaps you don't, your Dollie being so young yet."

Mrs Ellis smiled. "Dollie is a good girl," she said.

"Her father spoils her," said Mrs Gowland, acid.

Mrs Ellis bridled. "Now, Gladys, don't you say a word

against my Bert," she said. "Because I won't stand it. I won't really. I warn you."

"Of course it's p'raps natural, with Dollie coming so long after the boys," said Mrs Gowland nastily.

"That's nothing to do with you, Gladys, and I'll thank you to hold your tongue," said Mrs Ellis.

She spoke quite sharply, her fair pleasant face crimsoning.

"A silly name, Dollie, I always thought and still think," said Mrs Gowland, unable to resist firing a final shot. "Not 'with it' at all. Bert's fault, of course, I expect, always calling her Dollie."

"Gladys!" said Mrs Ellis in a warning tone, looking her sister-in-law firmly in the eye.

"Well, you know me. I always speak my mind."

"You do indeed."

"No offence, I hope."

"*I* hope none intended."

So much fight from a placid pussy like Dorothy Ellis was really alarming. Mrs Gowland thought it best to change the subject.

"Where's our train, I wonder?" she said, turning her sharp eyes around.

"It's not time for it for five minutes yet."

"There it is! Look! It's standing there outside the station."

"So it is," agreed Mrs Ellis. Her tone was mild; she was always ready for a reconciliation.

"What is it waiting for? Why doesn't it come to the platform, so we could get in and be comfortable?"

The seat they occupied had an open back. Mrs Ellis now turned a little, so that the other side of the platform came within her view.

A great many people stood there. Several, in fact many, were obviously business men of the "top" kind; executives, Mrs Ellis thought they called them. They wore heavy, well-cut topcoats of good West Riding cloth, with striped silk scarves and fur-lined leather gloves. They carried "real" leather brief-cases which looked heavy with papers, and appeared serious and concerned. One or two had secretaries with them; very bright young things, with abundant lustrous hair either very long and well-brushed, sweeping their shoulders, or gathered up tightly on their heads in complicated curls. Would Dollie look like that one day? Perhaps. The executives swung their brief-cases, examined their watches, and looked cross; the secretaries spoke soothingly, very competent about the time.

Among these business groups stood occasionally women; some of mature age in superb fur coats, obviously executive wives; some young, pretty, very much made up, hoping to become so. They wore charming, often brightly coloured clothes, some in trouser suits, some in mini-skirts, some in knee-length skirts which Mrs Ellis could not help preferring, some in long heavy coats. Their shoes or long boots, often patent leather (or at least looking like patent leather) were usually black or scarlet, and gleamed.

In a word, everybody on that side of the platform was wearing his or her best clothes. Mrs Ellis, who had known the bad times of the thirties, smiled at them benignly if with a certain wistfulness.

"They're waiting for the London train," she said.

Mrs Gowland whisked round and eyed them shrewdly.

"Yes! That's right!" she cried. "That's why our train doesn't come in. It's waiting for the London train to get in first. See! Look! That other line out there crosses our line. Of course they hold up the local train for the London train; they don't care two hoots about the local people."

"The people going to London are local too," murmured Mrs Ellis.

"If I had Lord Beeching here I'd tell him a few truths!"

"I'm sure you would, Gladys."

"They all look very well off," snarled Mrs Gowland.

"I daresay they work for it. And worry."

"Pooh!"

"And they're all going to London. They're in their best. We've only been shopping, think on."

"And had to carry our parcels up those awful steps!"

"There's a notice up saying passengers should ask porters for help with luggage and steps."

"What's the use of that when there's no porters? I don't see any porters carrying our parcels up those steps!"

"I believe there are lifts up from that passage underneath."

"I've never seen one. Have you?"

"Well, no. But that doesn't mean—" Mrs Ellis finished her sentence with a joyous cry: "But, see! There's one along there."

"It looks like it, certainly," said Mrs Gowland, grudgingly. Another woman might have agreed cheerfully: "So it is!" But that was not her way.

For a clash as of metal gates proved to be in fact the clack of one metal gate withdrawing into its appointed compartment. It slid back; an open space was revealed, shadowy in the distance; out of there a flat truck was emerging, laden with luggage; it rolled out, pushed by an elderly porter, rolled noisily but steadily along the platform on the London side, until it stood not three yards from Mrs Gowland and Mrs Ellis. They gazed at it. In fact, everybody gazed at it. The luggage on it was very handsome, four suitcases, all matching, black, with silvery locks and edges; obviously new.

"Looks new," observed Mrs Ellis in a low admiring tone.

"It does that. Somebody's got some money to spare, choose how," said Mrs Gowland, disagreeably envious.

At this point the elderly porter gave a slight twitch to the handle of the truck, which swung slowly on its axis, revealing what lay on the far side of one pair of suitcases. Mrs Gowland exclaimed. Mrs Ellis exclaimed. In fact, almost everybody on the platform exclaimed. Even the business men smiled a little beneath their well-groomed moustaches, though they turned away quickly so as not to betray their interest. For on the far side of the truck lay a superb pair of ladies' long boots. They were of suede; they had concealed zip fastenings, extremely neat; they were very long, oh, *very* long. And they were turquoise; yes, bright, fresh, new, beautiful turquoise.

"They're pale blue," whispered Mrs Ellis. "Though a deep colour in a way."

"Turquoise," snapped Mrs Gowland.

"Yes, turquoise," agreed Mrs Ellis.

"Well, as I say, some people have money to waste," commented Mrs Gowland.

"It's not waste, Gladys. Not those beautiful boots. At least we don't know it's waste."

"Whoever belongs to them, she shouldn't leave them lying about on a railway truck," criticised Mrs Gowland in an uncomfortably loud voice.

"We don't know," began Mrs Ellis.

"Encouraging people to steal, that's what I call it."

"Do you mean to steal the boots, Gladys?" enquired Mrs Ellis, vexed beyond bearing.

"Why, no, of course not, Dorothy," exclaimed Mrs Gowland.

The astonishment of her tone was justified, for Mrs Gowland's honesty, though perhaps she flaunted it a bit much, was permanent and sincere.

"Then why assume everybody else has a lower mind than you?"

The moment she had spoken Mrs Ellis was ashamed of herself; she felt she had been insulting. So she said hastily:

"Of course it *is* a bit risky, leaving boots like that on an open truck."

"Yes."

"The boots might fall off."

"Aye, and then somebody would be in trouble," said Mrs Gowland, recognising the olive branch but unable not to feel a little pleasure at the prospect of somebody in trouble.

"Exactly."

The two women exchanged friendlier glances. The elderly porter, not stirring a hair, continued to look straight ahead of him, but with a grim expression, which seemed to indicate that anyone trying to take those boots off his truck would have a tough job of it. All passengers present now discreetly withdrew their glances.

"It's interesting, though, the things you see at railway stations," murmured Mrs Ellis, turning away from the truck.

"I don't say otherwise," conceded Mrs Gowland.

At that very moment, two things happened.

In the distance, on the curve, majestically appeared the London train. Long, massive, with fresh paint gleaming, drawn by two powerful diesel engines, it swept at terrifying speed down towards the platform. Everyone stirred, looked alarmed or expectant, seized their hand luggage, stepped towards the edge of the platform, or in timidity back.

But their attention was distracted. For suddenly there burst into the crowd a rush of joyous young people. Young men in tail coats and grey waistcoats, with white roses in their buttonholes and a look of having left top hats outside; six young girls—yes, six, no fewer!—in the most delicious plain but well-cut thin white frocks—"They'll freeze," thought Mrs Ellis, alarmed for them—bands of roses in their hair, posies in their hands. One particularly handsome man, dark, tall, bright-eyed, slender—"Looks like a footballer or a cricketer or something," decided Mrs Ellis: "with those white roses, too." (The white rose being the Yorkshire symbol.) And one beautiful—oh, very beautiful—young girl; very fair, blue-eyed, beaming with happiness. "The bride, of course, they're a wedding party."

169

"I think I'll take these in the carriage with me," said the bride pleasantly, grasping the tops of the turquoise boots. The bridegroom politely took them from her.

And there was no doubt, of course, none at all, that the boots were hers, because her coat was of exactly the same delicious shade of turquoise as the boots. "A perfect match," thought Mrs Ellis with satisfaction.

The London train drew up. There was a good deal of fuss and excitement. Kisses, handshakes and confetti abounded. The elderly porter was so well tipped he beamed; at one moment it seemed as if the bride and bridegroom would miss the train, but the best man pushed them safely into their reserved seats. Everyone waved. The train moved away with dignity.

Meanwhile the little local train had backed quietly into the other side of the platform. Mrs Ellis and Mrs Gowland had hardly noticed its arrival, but now they heard porters shouting *Bradford, Hudley, Todmorden, Rochdale, Manchester* and hurriedly scrambled for it. The elderly porter pushed them in and slid the door closed; they sat down side by side with a bump; the train moved off.

"It makes you remember your own wedding, doesn't it?" murmured Mrs Ellis.

"It does *that*," said Mrs Gowland.

Her voice was muffled, and she was looking out of the window in a rather determined way. Mrs Ellis, surprised, gave her a glance and saw that there were actually tears in her eyes.

"She's not so bad, isn't old Gladys," thought Mrs Ellis sympathetically, "after all."

IN THE QUEUE

1971

MISS BEAMISH AND Mrs Lumb stood next to each other in the pension queue. They were, of course, both of pensionable age.

Miss Beamish sighed.

Mrs Lumb turned and looked at her.

Miss Beamish was tall and thin. She wore an old, shabby but neat navy blue coat and skirt, matching scarf, grey cotton gloves and a hat. A hat, thought Mrs Lumb in wondering contempt, laughing to herself; how ridiculous! Nobody wore hats nowadays. It was a small, dark, subdued, unnoticeable hat, to be sure; but still—a hat! Miss Beamish's thin, greying fair hair was stretched tightly back from her high forehead, and she wore old-fashioned spectacles. A clerk or a teacher or something dreary of that kind, thought Mrs Lumb; no need to see a ringless left hand to know *she* had never married. Still, there was something rather sweet in her expression; her face was faded, but it might have been rather pleasant when young. Good as gold, I expect, reflected Mrs Lumb bitterly. Nothing stand-offish about her, anyway. Her boy was killed in the Hitler war, p'raps. Mrs Lumb, oddly moved to friendliness, spoke.

"Allus a long queue for pensions," she said.

"Yes, indeed," agreed Miss Beamish in her gentle voice.

She looked at Mrs Lumb with interest. A plump, bosomy woman, wearing a slightly soiled orange (or perhaps it was meant to be pink?) cardigan and a tight black skirt. Her head scarf, very bright in shrill blue and green—were its colours what they called psychedelic?—had slipped from her head and lay in a crumpled mass round her strong white neck. Her short hair was very thick and dark, and tossed about her head in untidy waves, as though it had not felt a comb for weeks. Her face was lined but full of colour. A little too florid. Her eyes, however, were large, dark and rather fine. A handsome woman when young, I should think, reflected Miss Beamish, and an excellent mother—yes, I can see her with a lot of children who adored her. A rich, fine, useful life, full of work and love. A quiet, sad, wistful feeling, long suppressed, stirred Miss Beamish's heart; moved to friendliness, she smiled.

"And not much when we get it," pursued Mrs Lumb, encouraged.

"Better than nothing," said Miss Beamish, resigned.

"Well, yes. Of course," said Mrs Lumb, "I daresay if I didn't go out to work, I could get my rent paid by the Supplementary. Some do, you know."

"Do they really?"

"Oh, yes. But my old man, you see, he wouldn't like it."

"No," said Miss Beamish, sympathetic.

"But that isn't reely why I go out to work."

"No?"

"No. The thing is, you see, it's more cheerful."

"Ah!"

"I'm lonely, you see."

"I see," said Miss Beamish, who indeed knew all about loneliness.

"Well, you see, it's my old man. He's got arthritis, doesn't move except when he has to. He just sits there all day and night, and says nothing. Never has been one to talk. It was the same with the children. Play with them, yes, but talk to them, no. Before we were married, I thought he was the grandest man; I thought it was fine, the way he hardly ever said anything. I thought it was kind of proud and noble. But now, I'm tired of it. Yes, I'm tired of it. Do you know, I sit in the evening playing patience by myself on the table, and he never says a word. I'm tired of it. So I go out to work, you see, and it keeps me cheerful, like. I sit there playing patience of an evening, and he never says a word. I don't think he even sees what I'm doing. I don't. I don't reely."

"Oh, I don't think you should assume that," said Miss Beamish very seriously. "It's hardly fair to your husband to take his lack of interest in you for granted, is it?"

"Well, I don't know," said Mrs Lumb, opening her fine eyes wide as if surprised—she was really a bit stuck with that word *assume*. What did it mean exactly? Don't be so daft, she admonished herself; you understand what she means all right. "No, I don't think he takes a bit of notice of me nowadays, morning, noon or night, save when he needs his meals or his stick. We have one of those council flats, you know. High up. Very neat and all that, but you never see anybody. Across the way there's a young woman with a baby, her husband's a builder, you know, travels all over the country. She never comes in 'less she's short of sugar, something of that kind. I never speak to nobody when I'm home, so I go out to work, you see. 'Course, the money's useful. But if I stayed at home, I might get my rent paid. Some do. Or so I hear," she added, suddenly scrupulous for the truth.

The client at the counter walked away, the queue moved up, Miss Beamish and Mrs Lumb became involved in their financial affairs.

Next week, Miss Beamish and Mrs Lumb found themselves next to one another again in the queue. (No doubt, reflected Miss Beamish, their respective buses arrived in the town about the same time.) They were both dressed as before;

Mrs Lumb's abundant hair was, if anything, a trifle wilder. Miss Beamish smiled in a friendly style, but Mrs Lumb looked sour.

"I'm still going out to work," she said grimly, turning her head.

Miss Beamish looked interested. She was, indeed, keenly interested, but did not like to appear nosy by asking questions.

"I don't think he's said a word to me since I saw you last week," grumbled Mrs Lumb crossly.

"Really?" said Miss Beamish, shocked.

"Not one word. I might as well not be there at all."

"I hardly think," began Miss Beamish in a deprecating tone.

"No! He doesn't even see me. I'll tell you. Last night that young Mrs Whatnot from across the corridor suddenly banged on the door and burst in. It seems her mother is ill and she had to go home to her of a sudden, like—been ill a long time, it seems."

"Then it's not to be wondered at that she doesn't come in to have a word with you often," suggested Miss Beamish primly.

"That's right. Girl seems right enough, and a bit lonely like with her husband so much away. She had to run for her bus, so she asked us to give her husband a message when he came in—say she'd taken baby with her, and that, and he was to follow."

"You misjudged her," thought Miss Beamish, but did not like to say so.

"Happen I thought over harsh of her. But that's not the point. Point is, when she banged so hard on door, and burst in, I gave a start, like—"

"Very natural."

"Aye. And card I was holding flew out of my hand, and after she was gone I saw it had fallen against gas fire and

174

burned a corner off. We have North Sea gas, you know," said Mrs Lumb proudly, "and it's *hot*. Eh! What a do that was. Sixteen visits we had from one and another of them men before it went right. Still, it's settled down now, and it's *hot*. Corner of card were burned right off. Of course that's very awkward when you're playing patience, you know. I mean a patience where you lay a lot of cards out face down. If there's one with a corner off, you can't help knowing what it is."

"And was the burnt one a very important card?" enquired Miss Beamish.

"It were a black seven," said Mrs Lumb grimly. "As soon as you saw it, you couldn't help knowing what to do with it. While it was still face down, I mean. It was like cheating, if you see what I mean. I can't play patience with that pack honestly, any more."

"I'm very sorry," said Miss Beamish.

"Course, I went on about it a bit," admitted Mrs Lumb. "Anybody would. But did *he* tek notice? Not a ha'porth. Just sat there looking in front of him, not saying a word. I'm tired of it, I tell you, I'm right down fed up."

"I'm very sorry," said Miss Beamish humbly.

"Ha!" snorted Mrs Lumb. "So I'm still going out to work," she snapped, and she turned her back on Miss Beamish.

The following week, Miss Beamish was sorry to see that Mrs Lumb was not ahead of her in the queue, and—she looked carefully—not behind her either. Her nearest neighbour in the rear was a thin, stooping, grey-haired old man who sniffed a good deal. The queue at the next opening suddenly melted away rather fast, as sometimes happened when two or three applicants turned out to be together, and the rear of Miss Beamish's queue forsook it and joined this shorter line hopefully. Taught by bitter experience, however,

Miss Beamish and the thin grey man knew the disappointments of such a move, and remained faithful in their loyalty to their own line.

"Now then, lad!" came a loud cheerful voice in the rear. "Move off and let me come next to my friend."

"Nay, you're not jumping queue, surely," said the old man, pretending to be indignant.

"You can have your turn when we come to counter," said Mrs Lumb cheerfully. "I only want to be near my friend."

Miss Beamish looked round and saw Mrs Lumb. A much changed Mrs Lumb, however. The orange jumper had been washed, and now looked clearly pink; the black skirt had been sponged and pressed; the hair had been brushed and now showed its thick wave, lustrous and handsome. The face, too, was altogether different; the fine eyes sparkled, the red lips smiled.

"I shall be happy to make way for such a gradely lass, love," said the old man with a smile. He bowed and stepped back.

"Cheeky!" responded Mrs Lumb, laughing.

This swift flirtation had warmed the atmosphere of the entire post office; everyone looked round to enjoy it, and even the counter clerks smiled.

"Do you remember what I told you last week about a card getting its corner burned?" cried Mrs Lumb, poking Miss Beamish's hip sharply with her basket.

"I do indeed."

"Well, what do you think? When I got home that day, there was a new pack of cards waiting for me, on't table. A green rim they had, and gilt edges, and a picture of a girl at a spinning-wheel on the backs. All glossy. Oh, real posh! Must have cost a pretty penny."

"How delightful," began Miss Beamish.

"Fancy, he must have gone out with his stick and down in

the lift—he hates the lift—and crossed right across the road to buy them. 'T'isn't easy for him to walk out by himself now, you know," explained Mrs Lumb. "Arthritis. Yes. He must have gone out with his stick, while I was at work, you know, and down in the lift and right across the road. I was that flummoxed I couldn't find a word, at first, but then I said, 'Have you bought these for me, Schofield?' I said. Schofield's his first name, you know; the eldest son's always called Schofield in their family, traditional like. 'Have you bought these for me, Schofield?' I said. And he nodded."

"A nod is as good as a word," said Miss Beamish.

"It is *that* from him," said Mrs Lumb with emphasis. "So you see, I reckon he really took notice of me all the time. Like you said."

"Of course," said Miss Beamish, smiling with her head on one side.

"Aye, I reckon so. I reckon so, aye."

Miss Beamish's smile broadened.

"Whyn't you come up and see us some time?" urged Mrs Lumb, giving the address. She coloured and looked down, seeming rather embarrassed. "Just for a cuppa. Eh?"

"I shall be very happy to do so," said Miss Beamish, smiling with pleasure.

"Course, he may not say anything. But if he smiles, you won't mind him saying nowt?" urged Mrs Lumb.

"Of course not."

"Well, come on, lad, tek thi rightful place," shouted Mrs Lumb, hustling the thin old man one place up in the queue.

Miss Beamish, smiling happily, felt that her faith in human nature, married love, life itself, was restored.

FOR THE WEDDING

1971

THE PARKINS AND the Steads lived side by side, next door to each other, in a very respectable row. The houses had steps up to the front door, with porches, and a nice little square of garden.

Mr Parkin (Ted) was a foreman or floor manager or something of that sort at the big textile mill down the road. Mr Parkin was not tall, and though not plump, not thin— just comfortable, you might say. His hair, brownish-grey and not too tidy, was still abundant, and his dark grey eyes had a considerable twinkle. The mill thought the world of him; he had been there for years.

Mr Stead (James) was a different kind of man, a teacher, an English specialist at Rayburn Road Secondary Modern. He was tall and very lean, spectacled, balding and perhaps a little stooped, especially at the end of term, when he was tired. Shortly after he came to Rayburn Road, he was appointed deputy head teacher. There was a chance that he might get an appointment in the town as head teacher, but this did not come off. Mrs Parkin therefore privately thought him rather a softy, but this opinion was not shared by her daughter Lilian, who attended Rayburn Secondary Modern.

Thus, of the two men, Mr Parkin earned a good deal more, but Mr Stead had as it were more prestige.

Neither of the men was much for drinking. Mr Parkin— especially when exasperated by misconduct on the part of some piece (of cloth understood)—would occasionally pop into the Fleece at the end of the lane for a quick one; but Mr Stead, never. Not that he was a teetotaller or anything excessive of that kind; he just did not care much for pubs, so noisy and smoky; he preferred to have a quiet glass (just rarely) at home.

The great thing about Mr Parkin was his garden. Of course all Englishmen love their gardens, but Mr Parkin really had green fingers. With his jacket off and his braces taut over his shoulder, he could be seen any weekend, any evening, mowing, digging, tying, pruning. From February onward his border bloomed: snowdrops, crocus, daffodils, tulips (these grieved him because the sharp West Riding winds *would* cut their long stems), later lupins, delphiniums, hydrangeas, glorious roses. Mrs Parkin (her name was Lena) thought privately that Ted had a special eye for colour; she believed that in fact he would like to have been in a designer's office, playing about all day with coloured yarns.

But of course in their young days opportunities for such technical advancement were not easily come by, and there was the war, and their first child coming; when he got out of the army Ted took the first job he could get. He never said a word about designing, of course; he wasn't that kind of man; but Lena knew. Oh, *she* knew.

Now Mr Stead (James), though no doubt he was right book-learnéd, admitted Mrs Parkin, had no gift at all for gardening. He admired Mr Parkin's garden enormously, asked his advice and took it, and really did his best; but, poor fellow, somehow his plants never succeeded. They were thin and weedy, with miserable little blooms, and as for his roses, they always caught greenfly or mildew or both, so that at last he gave them up.

"Unfair on them," he said. Mrs Parkin thought this rather daft and far-fetched, but Mr Parkin understood and nodded gravely.

Mr Parkin had been stationed in the north of Scotland during the war; he made good friends there, the Parkins often holidayed there when the war was over, and the result of this was that their son John Edward married a Scots girl and was happily settled up there. Then quite a few years later, unexpectedly the Parkins had another child, a girl, whom they called Lilian. Coming late and surprisingly as she did, a kind of bonus, naturally Ted and Lena doted on Lilian.

Apart from that, she was a lovely girl. Really pretty. Lovely fair hair, really golden—"My mother had fair hair," explained Mrs Parkin, for her own hair was just light brown. Lilian had beautiful blue eyes. A complexion as pure as snow, only warmer. A sweet face. A sweet disposition too, though not a softy, and quite clever in a quiet way. She did reasonably well at school, attended the local technical college and took a secretarial course and obtained a very nice job in a lawyer's office. Meanwhile, interestingly enough, the Steads had rather the same experience. They too had two children, but the elder was a girl, married to a teacher and living in London. Mrs Stead too had been a teacher before her marriage. In truth Mrs Parkin was rather overawed by all this teacher business, and London and what have you—she found Mrs Stead rather stiff, and suspected that Mrs Stead found her gossipy. However, the Steads were good neighbours; very honest and considerate. When their second child, Robert his name was, a rampageous noisy lad if ever there was one, with red hair—yes, really red, carrotty—broke one of the Parkins's windows with a misplaced football, Mr Stead brought him in to admit the fault and apologise, and paid for the window at once. Robert attended Rayburn Road school, of course. When he left he got himself apprenticed in a large engineering works. He came home at night looking dirty but cheerful, and was said to be doing well.

Well, then, all of a sudden came a bombshell. One evening when Lilian was out with a friend of hers at the pictures, or so Mrs Parkin thought, there were voices at the door and in came Lilian, radiant, with Robert Stead at her side. Mr Parkin had gone out for one of his rare drinks, and Mrs Parkin was alone. It was summer, and she was sitting in the front room, looking out at the flowers. She gazed at Robert Stead in astonishment. He had been a tiresome carrotty teen-ager for so long that she was astounded to see him as a young man, quite tall, quite good-looking now that his hair was brushed and he was out of his overalls and clad in a hand-some pullover and some decent dark slacks.

"You remember Bob, mother," said Lilian rather im-patiently.

Mrs Parkin gasped.

"Robert Stead, Mrs Parkin," announced the young man. "I was hoping to see Mr Parkin but I can tell you instead, can't I. Lilian and I have decided to get married, so we'd like to get engaged now."

Mrs Parkin gave a dumbfounded gurgle.

"I shall be out of my apprenticeship next year," went on Robert. "I've been saving quite a while, and there's hope of some rooms in Back Rayburn Street—of course, we'll put our names down for a Council House, but what a hope!"

Mrs Parkin continued to gape.

"Well, I'll leave you to think it over, Mrs Parkin," said Robert cheerfully.

He kissed Lilian in a determined and somehow accustomed way, thought Mrs Parkin mournfully, and strode out.

"Now, mother, love, don't take on," said Lilian, kissing her. "It can't have come as a surprise to you, really."

"Yes, it has," wept Mrs Parkin. "Of course, love, it may be just a passing fancy, you know."

"Nonsense!" said Lilian robustly. "We were reported twice about it, before we left school."

"Reported for what?" cried Mrs Parkin, horrified.

"Oh, just talking alone in the library," returned Lilian, cool.

"I hope there's nothing *wrong*!" gasped Mrs Parkin.

"Of course not, mother," said Lilian angrily. "We're not the permissive sort."

The sound of Mr Parkin's key in the front latch was heard.

"Well, go up to bed, Lily, love," implored Mrs Parkin. "Here's your father."

"Will you tell him, or shall I?" pressed Lilian. "Or Bob could come back if I asked him—"

"*I*'ll tell your father."

"He won't need much telling, I think," said Lilian, laughing as she slipped away upstairs.

Mrs Parkin groaned.

"What on earth's the matter?" cried Mr Parkin, alarmed by his wife's tearstained face.

"Oh, Ted! Here's Lilian and that Bob next door wanting to get engaged."

"Tell me summat new," said Mr Parkin, sitting down to remove his shoes.

"Did you—know?"

"Let's say I've seen it coming."

"Oh, Ted!"

"What's the fuss about? He's a good lad, she's known him long enough to know whether she likes him, by next year he'll be a tradesman with a skill in his fingers, I reckon they love each other. You couldn't wish for better in-laws than the Steads."

At first Mrs Parkin's disappointment at the engagement was, let's face it, acute. But—perhaps it was odd, perhaps it was just human nature—she revived considerably when she found that Mrs Stead was disappointed too.

"Really, you might think Mrs Stead thought our Lilian not good enough for their Robert," she said indignantly to her husband.

"I expect she does. Very natural," rejoined Ted.

"Our Lilian! Not good enough for that rough red-haired chap!"

"Bob's as dear to his parents as Lilian is to hers."

"Well! If Mrs Stead is trying to break up their engagement, she can think again, that's all!" fulminated Mrs Parkin. "Our Lily! So good and beautiful! They're promised! She's given him her heart! Let Mrs Stead just try, that's all! I'll see to that, I can tell you!"

"I'm sure you're right, love," murmured Ted.

The affianced year passed; Robert came out of his apprenticeship and got himself quite a good job. How Mrs Parkin managed to boast about this job to her circle of friends, while continuing to regard Bob with all the contempt due from a mother-in-law, it is difficult to say. But she did. That is, until the wedding was actually in sight, when she suddenly found herself, not exactly opposed, but slightly hung up, about the arrangements by a coolness—it was no more, but she felt it—on Mrs Stead's part. The wedding reception was to be held in the Sunday school, with catering from the Fleece at so much a head.

"My daughter and her husband will be coming from London. I hope that is—all right," murmured Mrs Stead.

"Of course," said Mrs Parkin. "Our John Edward and Alison and the new baby will be coming down from Glasgow. We want our families about us at these times."

"Indeed, yes. But we must not—overburden—your list of guests unduly."

"Oh, don't worry about that!" said Mrs Parkin robustly. "Ted will be equal to anything of that kind, I assure you."

She respected the Steads' consideration in this respect, but found its manner a bit chilly. Why not speak straight out?

Then Mrs Stead seemed not to want to have beer or port or any drink of that kind to be served at the reception. Mrs Parkin's eyes opened as wide as saucers. "Oh, but we must," she said. Ted agreed with her and the point was settled. But the Steads were cool.

However, the minister agreed to perform the ceremony, the banns were put in, the bridesmaids—a cousin on each side and a couple of tiny tots from colleagues and friends—selected. A friend of Lilian's, a considerable seamstress, promised to make the wedding garments. She was a joyful girl who liked clothes to be "with it". Mrs Stead smiled at the styles chosen affably, but not with warmth. On the evening when a consultation had revealed this coolness, Lilian was observed to be looking downhearted; she even had tears in her eyes.

"What's the matter, love?" enquired Mrs Parkin tenderly, putting an arm round her daughter's shoulders. "It is Bob?"

"No, no. It's never Bob," said Lilian, weeping. "It's just I'm a bit worried about the wedding."

The truth was that while Lilian loved her mother heartily and knew her goodness and kindness of heart, she was not blind to her defects. Mrs Parkin's voice was often loud, her manner was sometimes abrupt and off-putting—she spoke her mind, as she often said—and her taste in colours was garish. Mrs Stead on the other hand was almost too quiet and retiring. If there was to be some awful clash about the wedding! Bob, who loved his mother dearly, would be upset . . . Oh dear!

"I don't think Mrs Stead likes those sleeves," wept Lilian.

"If you don't want those sleeves, love, you shan't have them," said Mrs Parkin emphatically. "I'll run round and tell Doreen. I'll take it on myself. I'll say I find, on thinking it over, you know, I don't like them."

"Will you, mother?" murmured Lilian gratefully between sniffles.

The sleeves were altered.

When this incident was told to Ted, he mused a while, then said:

"Where are you getting *your* gear for the wedding, then, Lena? Eh?"

Mrs Parkin named a bustling establishment. "I haven't got round to it yet, with one thing and another," she said, "I must go tomorrow."

"I think you'd better go to Madam Darcy," said Ted.

"What!"

"Aye. Why not? She's a good sort."

"She's an old flame of yours, I know that, in her young days before she got so smart. But nowadays! The price, Ted! The cost! Madam Darcy! She's the best shop in town."

"I'll bet Mrs Stead'll go there."

"Well—"

"You've no need to worry, Lil love," Mrs Parkin told her daughter, who, working every day, was not easily available for shopping. "I've got the most lovely pink outfit at Madam Darcy's."

Pink! Lilian could have screamed, moaned, but settled for a laugh. Pink was a beautiful shade, discreetly handled. But her mother's views on pink! The outfit—horrid word—would be loud and awful. Well, all right, it'll be awful, said Lilian staunchly. Mrs Steed will be inexpensive and elegant, and poor old Mum will be costly and awful. The Steads and the Parkins have got to learn to put up with each other—Dad and Mr Stead manage well enough, choose how, and we've got to do the same. She faced the agony she would endure at the wedding, and fought it down, and said nothing about it to anybody, just kept it in her heart rather warmly. As the wedding approached, she looked a trifle pale—which was natural—but she had never looked more beautiful.

"Our Lil's a lovely lass," said Mrs Parkin, tender.

"She's growing up," said Mr Parkin with satisfaction.

"And what have you two fathers been nattering about, down at the Fleece together? I never heard of such a thing!"

Mrs Parkin rallied him, laughing. "I thought his lordship never went to a pub, ha ha !'

"Now, mother," said Ted. "James Stead is a very fine fellow in his quiet way, and I enjoy talking to him."

"But what do you find to talk *about*?"

"Oh, just a quiet natter," said Ted mildly.

The wedding day arrived. There was the usual fuss and flutter. Mum ran about from floor to floor. Would the flowers come? Would old auntie turn up in time? (John Edward and family had arrived the night before.) The taxis! The taxis! They would be late! No, they were here, but mum and auntie were not ready! Yes, they were. Alison tucked them in. Where was Dad's buttonhole? Oh, he was wearing it. Where was the second baby bridesmaid? The first adult bridesmaid's dress was too tight round the waist. Scissors were used on a gusset. The second baby arrived crying, but recovered. Dad and Lilian set off too early— this was Lilian's fault. Bob had said the night before: "Don't keep me waiting, Lil. I couldn't bear it." So they arrived at the chapel early. But what did it matter? There was a bustle of people in the porch. Bridesmaids and their mammas; John Edward, Alison, Baby; the headmaster, one or two other belated guests; Mr and Mrs Stead, Mrs Parkin and auntie.

"Well, you two ladies certainly harmonise most beautifully," said the headmaster. "A delightful picture."

Lilian, looking at Bob's mother and her own, almost fainted with astonishment. Mrs Stead, pale and slim, with beautifully groomed white hair, was deliciously elegant in palest pink. Mrs Parkin, glowing and bosomy, looked vividly handsome in deep dark rich rose. As the headmaster said, they harmonised. Their pinks were in the same "range" of colour. They made a delightful picture together.

"More by good luck than management, I'm afraid,"

boomed Mrs Parkin happily. "I just fell in love with this at . . ."

"It shows we have the same kind of taste basically," said Mrs Stead in her light pretty voice, not listening.

They went off together into the chapel, smiling.

"Daddy," said Lilian faintly. She put her hand within his arm and looked up at him.

He smiled down, squeezed her hand and gave her the biggest wink she had ever seen on a human face.

The wedding march sounded and they paced down the aisle together.

REMOVAL

1971

"WELL, HERE WE are then," said Mrs Thorpe in a tone of doom, proffering one of those official, close-typed, long-paragraphed letters which strike fear to the heart of the ordinary housewife. "This is what they're offering me. A high-rise flat, believe it or not."

"Where is it?" faltered her employer, diffident about this matter, so important to her housekeeper.

"Ninth floor, Rutland Court. Fancy me living in a Court! But why Rutland? It's a very un-Yorkshire name, is that. Rutland, indeed!"

"It may be an improvement on your present home," suggested Miss Ellis.

Mrs Thorpe lived in the middle of a terrace facing the long blank wall of a mill. The house was still sturdy, but having been built some hundred and twenty years, it lacked indoor sanitation and other amenities.

"I've lived there all my married life and some years after," growled Mrs Thorpe. "I don't want to change. Of course," she added, almost killing herself in the attempt to be fair, "Rutland is convenient for the bus, I don't deny. But what's the sense of this new road they're building? Knocking everything down! Do you see any sense in it?"

"Well, not much. When shall you inspect the Rutland flat?"

"This afternoon. If I don't like it I shan't accept it, choose what they say."

"May I come with you?"

"Why not? Though you don't know much about housing," said Mrs Thorpe frankly.

The caretaker of Rutland Court, who met them in the foyer, proved to be an active kindly man in his late thirties. He explained the mysteries of doors and lifts and keys.

"You've got a telephone here, I see," said Mrs Thorpe, advancing towards the box.

"It's not installed yet," said the caretaker hastily.

Mrs Thorpe snorted.

They ascended to the ninth floor.

"How beautifully clean!" exclaimed Miss Ellis, enjoying the white walls.

"The walls are clean but the floor isn't," said Mrs Thorpe.

"That's easily remedied," said the caretaker.

"What a superb view!" exclaimed Miss Ellis, gazing out of the large windows while Mrs Thorpe inspected the rooms.

The whole of Hudley lay on the sloping hillside below them; the cars and vans and buses seemed toylike and harmless from this height, their colours bright in the sunshine, with little coloured toy people skipping about safely between them. In the distance, across the valley, rose Awe Hill, on the crest of which a beacon pan had been erected in the days of Queen Elizabeth I, to warn the town of the coming of the Armada. Miss Ellis mentioned this.

"It didn't come, though," said Mrs Thorpe at her side, with satisfaction. "The kitchen isn't bad," she added, "and the bathroom is really rather sweet—neat, I mean," she substituted hastily.

The caretaker beamed.

"But of course," went on Mrs Thorpe, feeling, it was clear, she had been too easily pleased: "that narrow shelf over the electric radiator, I don't like that. My cats won't like that, for sure."

"Cats!" exclaimed the caretaker in horror. "You can't keep pets here, missis."

"My cats are made of china," Mrs Thorpe told him haughtily.

"Oh, well—that's different. China cats'd fit on that shelf nicely. Give it a homely look, like."

"Bingo wouldn't. He's too big. His tail would hang over."

"Put him on top of the Telly, love."

"Bingo doesn't like the Telly. He scorns it."

"Fancy saying a pot cat scorns T.V.," murmured the caretaker to Miss Ellis, as Mrs Thorpe inspected the bathroom once again.

"I think that was meant as a joke," hazarded Miss Ellis.

"I wondered at the time, but I didn't feel I knew her well enough to risk a laugh. Have you known her long?"

"About twenty-five years," replied Miss Ellis, offhand.

The caretaker nodded and seemed pleased.

Two days later Mrs Thorpe burst in with Miss Ellis's breakfast tray, beaming.

"I've done it!" she announced.

"What?"

"I signed for the flat."

"I'm sure you've been wise."

"You don't think it was kind of cold and unhomely?"

"There's nothing in it yet to make it homely."

"That's right. It'll be all right—"

"—when you get your cats in."

They laughed together.

A period of some tension and anxiety followed. Papers had to be signed, fittings chosen. A few rails and hooks were necessary—but it appeared permission had to be asked before the sacred walls could be subjected to such invasions.

"I don't know what this country's coming to, really. If

you've to ask permission to put up a rail! Upon my word!"

The great difficulty was the divan. The Hudley furniture shops abounded in divans, but they all had three seats.

"But what is your objection to a three-seater, Mrs Thorpe?" pleaded Miss Ellis.

"It won't go in! Well, it would but there wouldn't be room for two chairs as well. And people *will* drop in, you know."

However, all of a sudden the tide turned. Mrs. Thorpe was a member of a large and flourishing family, and had the crowd of friends her staunch and generous nature deserved. Every one of these relatives and friends turned up to help in the removal. A sister found a two-seater divan! ("The shop was having a sale, and she saw a lot of people going in.") Another sister helped to choose and measure carpets. A niece made and hung matching curtains. A great-nephew arrived with tools to put up hooks and rails. ("He's quite handy with his hands, is our Thomas, though he's at University really.")

Gifts poured in. From a biscuit barrel to a broom, from matching soap to an electric kettle, from cushions to a bed-side lamp.

"I should like a pouffe, really," said Mrs Thorpe in a wistful tone.

"A pouffe!"

"To sit on, you know. Or put your feet up. They take up very little room—you can put them away underneath a table."

"I don't think I've seen one lately."

"Some are leather—well, pretend to be leather—and some are silk, or chintz, you know."

It turned out that our so-and-so who was leaving Hudley to live with a married daughter in London owned a pouffe; having observed Mrs Thorpe's admiration, she had it re-covered and offered it with becoming diffidence.

And so at last everything was complete, and Miss Ellis went to Rutland Court for a cup of tea. Everything was really perfect; Bingo slept comfortably, tail out-curved, on a finely knitted blue mat on the Telly; mats, rugs, curtains, towels, upholstery, all matched in the most tasteful style; flowers decked a table in the hall, china gleamed, cushions were fresh and plump. Miss Ellis admired it all whole-heartedly.

"You have made it a real home," she said.

But Mrs Thorpe's ethics forbade her to accept a personal compliment. A rebuke, she felt, was necessary.

"There's a beautiful view," she said sternly.

"Good," approved Miss Ellis.

MOTHER-IN-LAW

1974

I T   W A S   F R I D A Y . Mrs Blacker, grey-haired, widowed,
old-age pensioner, wearing her decent coat and hat and
carrying her new striped nylon shopping bag, unlatched the
gate on the trim little council house rented by her son Ronnie
and his wife Lucy.

She had come, as usual on Fridays, to wash up, clean the
house, do the week's shopping, cook an evening meal and
share it with Ronnie and Lucy. This was all very helpful, for
Lucy, who taught in the same secondary-modern school as
her husband, was as conscientious and enthusiastic a teacher
as Ronnie, and extra activities for her pupils gave her very
little time for domestic duties.

Mrs Blacker, as usual, walked sedately up the trim little
path. But here the course of events departed from the usual,
for the trim white door was vigorously thrown open by
Lucy, who then stood back to allow Ronnie, who came rushing down the stairs, to bound over the two outside steps and
charge towards the gate.

"Mom! Train!" he cried as he flew past.

Mrs Blacker was naturally a little perturbed, but not
seriously so, for Ronnie's pleasant face—he had a thick
thatch of fair hair, with fair complexion to match—wore a
look of happy excitement. This agreeable impression was
confirmed by the appearance of Lucy, who now stood visible
in the open doorway, beaming.

"Mother!" she exclaimed. Mrs Blacker always winced a little when Lucy called her *Mother*, but she approved the motive and concealed the wince. Soon, she hoped, the appellation *Grannie* would become applicable. There had been no announcement yet, but Mrs Blacker's hopes were strong. "He's short-listed for Annotsfield!" cried Lucy.

"How splendid!" cried Mrs Blacker.

She had heard nothing of the appointment in question, but knew from experience of Ronnie's teaching posts, what a "short-list" meant.

"Yes. We didn't tell you he's applied—we didn't tell anybody except our head teacher," said Lucy, panting just a trifle from embarrassment. "Because it's not wise for too many applications to get around, if they're not successful, you know."

"No, indeed," agreed Mrs Blacker loyally. But she was wounded. "Not tell his own mother," she mourned to herself. To conceal any awareness of the slight, she took off her hat and coat, and hung them up, with the shopper, behind the door.

"The letter summoning him for an interview came this morning. Fancy his being on the short list for the first headship he's applied for!" marvelled Lucy.

"He's a wonderful boy. And you're such a help to him in his career, Lucy," said Mrs Blacker, generous as usual.

Lucy kissed Mrs Blacker.

"He's catching the five past nine train to Annotsfield. He expects to be back this evening. Why not sit a moment and have a cup of coffee, Mother?" urged Lucy happily.

Mrs Blacker's digestion, soothed by nearly seventy years of tea, shuddered at the thought of coffee, which did not agree with her. (She suspected that it did not agree too well with Ronnie, either.)

"No, thank you, dear," she said cheerfully. "I'd rather get on with the house."

194

"Well, I must be off." said Lucy, bustling about for coat and briefcase. "I must give the head time to rearrange the time-table in Ronnie's absence today, before prayers. Luckily I have a free period this morning, so I'll be available to substitute for Ronnie then."

"Shall you be in for lunch?" said Mrs Blacker, making the effort to use for this midday meal the word preferred by Lucy.

"I'm not sure—probably not," said Lucy, rushing out.

Mrs Blacker cleared the breakfast things, got out the vacuum—yes they had a vacuum, she was proud to know, paid for too—and cleaned the house from top to toe. It was not a tiresome task, for Lucy was a very tidy person; all clothes were neatly put away in drawers and cupboards, and dressing-table and sideboard fitments were geometrically arranged. Mrs Blacker took great pains to memorise the positions of these and replace them exactly. When Ronnie and Lucy first married and she began these Friday visitations, she had not troubled about this overmuch, for though she kept her own home scrupulously tidy, she ordered it by instinct rather than by calculation. But one Friday evening she saw Lucy, with a tiny frown of vexation, alter the relative position of two ornaments on the mantelpiece. Mrs Blacker took the hint, and since then she had never left anything out of place.

Mrs Blacker liked using the vacuum. It was efficient, easy, and she enjoyed following the edges of carpets and chairs exactly. There was something playful in this exactitude which pleased her robust and cheerful nature. But more than this, its drone made a protective barrier between herself and the outside world. Within it she was free to dream. Now, with this splendid news about Ronnie's short-listing to set her off, she began to re-live her life since his birth.

A strong, beautiful, healthy boy, he very soon developed a most deliciously friendly and interested expression in his

fine dark-blue eyes. Was Jim proud of him! Ah, well; Jim.
Best not to think of Jim; the old wound, the piercing grief,
was still there. Jim came back safely through the war,
Dunkirk and all, only to die of rheumatic fever before
Ronnie was ten years old. Jim was most terribly proud of
Ronnie.

"He's a clever boy, a right down clever lad, is our Ronnie,"
he said. "He's far above our heads, Cissie love." (Jim was a
warehouseman in a textile merchants' firm; nicely paid and
a clean job, but not, of course, like a teacher.) "We must
do all we can for Ronnie."

Cissie agreed with all her heart, and after she had lost
Jim, Ronnie became the great motive, the moving passion,
of her life. Of course in these modern times, with grants and
exams and what not, and Ronnie up to all of them, it was
not too difficult to get him the education he wanted. All
the same, it was hard work. Ronnie had to play games, of
course, like other boys, and go camping and so on. So there
were football boots, blazers, gym shoes, and all that; and
how that boy ate, how he grew out of his clothes! Jim had
been just medium size, but Mrs Blacker's family came
bigger, and Ronnie was a fine figure of a lad, tall and broad,
though lean. Mrs Blacker went out as a daily woman, five
days a week, for twelve years. It came hard on her particularly, because living with her old widowed mother she had
a bedridden invalid on her hands as well, to care for. Ronnie
took a newspaper-round and ran errands, which helped, but
it was hard. Then her mother died and pensions came in,
so things were easier.

Mrs Blacker wanted Ronnie to go to university, as they
said nowadays, and everyone told her he could easily do
it, but Ronnie said no.

"I'm going to a training college," he said, "and I'll be at
work this time year after."

Mrs Blacker expostulated, argued. Not that she knew much

about what it all meant, but other people occasionally told her.

"Shut up, Mom," said Ronnie firmly at last. "I'm not your blue-eyed little boy any more. I'm a man and I must do things my own way. You've had enough of working for me. It's time I began to work for you, for a change."

The words were rough, but his tone was extremely tender—after all, he was a Yorkshireman, like his father.

"You're a good son, Ronnie," said Mrs Blacker, tears in her eyes.

"Ha! Can't say I've noticed it," said Ronnie sardonically.

So he went to a training college and soon began to teach.

In his first job he was not altogether content. Not that he ever had any trouble with his pupils, either boys or girls; with them everything went as it should. But the head teacher was rather frustrating.

"He's a good man in his way," said Ronnie. "But facing back instead of forward."

However, he soon got another job, under a very forward-looking man this time. Now he was happy; everything went swimmingly; he worked extremely hard, he took courses; he was dedicated to the life of the school; he liked all the teachers and they liked him. Soon the job of deputy head fell vacant, and he got it as everyone knew he would.

The only thing which worried Mrs Blacker at this time was the number of pretty young women teachers who flocked around him. Of course Mrs Blacker wished her son to marry, but was anxious he should find the right wife.

"Do be careful amongst all those young girls, Ronnie," she said.

"It's an occupational hazard, Mom," said Ronnie, laughing. "I'm on my guard."

Sure enough it was three years before he suddenly became at first rather quiet, then rather snappy, then brought Lucy to tea on Sunday afternoon. On this occasion he was beamingly happy, and Lucy was beamingly happy too. When consulted, Mrs Blacker gave warm approval to their betrothal and marriage. It was obvious, thought Mrs Blacker, that they were made for each other. If she was a little afraid of Lucy, a trifle chilled, what mother-in-law did not feel the same? But Lucy was just the right girl for a head-teacher's wife, no doubt about that. She was dark and slender, not pretty but distinguished-looking; she was clever, she was well read, she was a history specialist, she cared for her pupils just as Ronnie did; she loved him (it was obvious) dearly. She spoke well, with a good accent; her dress, though quiet and inexpensive, was always agreeable and neat. She always had herself well under control. Mrs Blacker saw at once that she could not come to live with Lucy and Ronnie, though Ronnie pressed it; but Lucy without doubt was just the right girl for a head-teacher's wife. And here was Ronnie already on a short list for a headship!

Of course one could not expect him to succeed the first time. Mrs Blacker had the impression that it was usually about the third application which succeeded. But succeed he would; he was all set to lead a happy, useful, successful life. Mrs Blacker was in the couple's bedroom now. The vacuum droned, Mrs Blacker smiled; the noise seemed a purr of happiness in her happy world.

Suddenly she started.

"Lucy!" she exclaimed.

Lucy, the sound of whose footsteps had of course been drowned by the vacuum, stood in front of her, panting, a look of anxiety on her pointed little face.

Mrs Blacker switched off at once.

"Is there anything wrong?"

"No—I forgot to give you the shopping list, that's all," said Lucy. "In the excitement of getting Ronnie off for his train." She laughed.

"But won't you be home for—lunch?"

"No. I'm taking Ronnie's lunch duty. So I've just dashed home in break time. Here's the list."

Mrs Blacker took the quarter-sheet of paper, neatly inscribed, as usual, with all the quantities carefully listed beside the groceries.

"I'll just get the money for you," said Lucy, hurrying to the dressing-table. She pulled open a top drawer.

There was a silence. Mrs Blacker stood expectant.

At last Lucy turned. Her face, a moment ago flushed from her hurry, was now pale, drawn, and, Mrs Blacker could not help feeling, somehow hostile.

"Have you been into this drawer, Mrs Blacker?" said Lucy quietly.

"Me?" said Mrs Blacker, dumbfounded. "Of course not! I never go into your drawers or cupboards, Lucy."

"Oh. Well. Of course not. Here are the notes for the shopping," said Lucy. "Give me the list a moment, please. I'll change it."

She took the paper from her mother-in-law's hand, and with a few well-chosen alterations, as the experienced housewife Mrs Blacker clearly saw, knocked nearly a pound's expenditure off the list.

The Town Hall clock struck. Lucy with a harassed exclamation rushed down the stairs and left the house. She did not bang the front door, for Lucy never banged doors, but she closed it with some determination.

Mrs Blacker stood gaping in the middle of the bedroom floor, with the shaft of the vacuum cleaner in her hand. What? How? Why? What was all that about? She pondered. Suddenly she understood. Lucy thought that she, Mrs Blacker, Ronnie's mother, had opened Lucy's drawer and stolen a pound note.

Blood rushed to her face. She stamped her foot in rage. The shaft of the vacuum cleaner fell heavily to the ground. She kicked it as it lay. Lucy! That thin, pinched, mean, breastless (Mrs Blacker was a full-bosomed woman), plain, arrogant, affected creature had dared to think an accusation of dishonesty against her! Against Mrs Blacker, who had never stolen or misused a ha'penny in her life! Against Ronnie's mother! It was insufferable, it was intolerable, it was beyond bearing! She had always felt that Lucy was unworthy of Ronnie. Hateful creature! She loathed her! What would the children of such a woman be? A frightful vista suddenly opened before her of a couple of pale, mean-minded, ugly children with suspicious natures and superior smiles, whose conduct would lacerate Ronnie's warm generous heart. Well, that should not happen. She would separate Ronnie from his odious wife. She had only to tell him of Lucy's detestable suspicion to turn him against her for ever. An accusation against Ronnie's mother! Who had brought him up through all these years of hardship! Who had loved and cherished him, sacrificed for him, given up everything for him! (She remembered fleetingly Jack Tolson, who had wanted to marry her in her widowhood, but of course she had refused.)

"The very minute Ronnie enters this house I'll tell him. And then we shall see."

She wound up the flex of the vacuum and put it angrily in the cupboard, dusted the furniture and replaced it exactly in the room.

It was now time for her midday meal, but after taking out a snack of bread and cheese, she suddenly threw it back into the cupboard, finding it impossible to eat anything which belonged even partly to Lucy. Instead, she inserted Lucy's pound notes into her purse with hands that trembled with fury, put on her hat and coat, took down her shopper from the back of the door, and left the house. As she walked down the hill to the town she went over and over again in her mind the speech she meant to make to Ronnie.

"Your wife thinks your mother stole a pound note. What do you think of that?"

Her face was crimson, her heart pounded, every fibre of her body seethed with pain.

She began to make the required purchases with meticulous care, writing down the price of each in large angry figures, opposite the items in Lucy's list.

It was when she placed her first purchase in her striped shopper, her shopping bag, that a small qualm assailed her. With the second purchase the qualm was sharper. With the third it really hurt. With the fourth it was unbearable.

The qualms were the fault of the shopper. Ronnie had given her the striped shopper a week or two ago, to replace her old basket.

"Baskets are out, Mom," he said, laughing. "You must keep up to date, you know. You must be with it. Nylon shoppers are all the go, nowadays. Seriously, Mom," he added, spreading the shopper's plastic handles wide to show its capacity, "this will be easier for you. Less bumpy. Lighter. More flexible."

Always such a good son, Ronnie. Thoughtful. Observant. All that about baskets being unfashionable at the moment was nonsense, of course. He had simply noticed that her basket was growing hairy and feeble, indeed had been mended with string. He wished to replace it without wounding her pride, without appearing to give her anything. Mrs Blacker emphatically did not want her son to be always giving her things, as if she were a poor relation. Mrs Blacker's independence was, she freely admitted, quite ferocious. Yes, Ronnie was kindness itself. He really loved his mother. He would be furious when he learned of his wife's accusation. He would be furious. Yes, he would be furious. His fresh, pleasant, happy face would change, would darken and sadden, would harden and chill. For the first time it occurred to Mrs Blacker to consider, not how she would feel, but how

Ronnie would feel, when he heard of his wife's accusation. A boy so sensitive to a decrepit basket obviously felt everything very strongly. The accusation would make him unhappy. When you came to think of it, he would never be quite as happy again. Of course he wouldn't believe Lucy's accusation for a moment, Mrs Blacker was sure of that. He had been through too much with his mother, knew her too well. But what would he think of the wife who had made such a charge? He would feel deeply grieved, even angry, bitterly disappointed in any case, to be unable to trust his wife to feel as he did. Yes, bitterly disappointed to be unable to trust his wife.

And was she really planning to destroy her son's happiness in this way? Did she really intend to introduce the worm of distrust into his heart?

All these years she had worked for him, cared for him; was she now to tarnish his married happiness? From disappointment it was but a step to resentment, to feeling estranged, misunderstood. Was Ronnie's mother to—No.

"No," thought Mrs Blacker, closing the handles of the shopper firmly as the last parcel went in. "No. Certainly *not.*"

"But Lucy'll tell him," she thought as she toiled wearily up the hill. "She'll tell him tonight, when they're alone. Well, that's her look-out. If she does, she'll spoil their marriage. I won't, choose how."

When she reached Ronnie's house, she found the lights on, the coke fire red hot (they were in a smokeless zone), the cups and saucers on the table, and Lucy putting on the kettle. Her daughter-in-law ran to her and took the striped nylon shopper quickly out of her hand. Mrs Blacker was panting a little.

"You haven't walked all the way up the hill with this heavy bag?" exclaimed Lucy reproachfully. Mrs Blacker nodded. "But why?"

"I never thought of the bus."

Lucy exclaimed again—but rather artificially, Mrs Blacker thought.

"How can I warn her to say nothing about the pound note to Ronnie?" she wondered, emptying the shopper. "If I say anything, she'll think I'm pleading for myself."

Anger rose in her again at this thought, and she glanced sharply at Lucy. To her surprise, her daughter-in-law's eyelids appeared reddened, as if she had been weeping. "Maybe she's troubled too," thought Mrs Blacker.

"You're home early," she said in a friendlier tone.

"I came straight from school," said Lucy, mentioning the various out-of-school activities she had skipped. "I wanted to be home for Ronnie, in case he should catch an earlier train."

"Ah," said Mrs Blacker, nodding thoughtfully. "Now for it," she told herself. "This is the best chance you'll get." She summoned all her courage, raised her head, and gazing straight into Lucy's fine grey eyes, said meaningfully: "Ronnie."

Into her glance, her tone, she threw everything she had ever felt or meant—Jim, Ronnie as a baby, a boy, a lad, a man, her love for him, her hopes and fears for his future, his need of silence. "Ronnie," she said again.

"Ronnie," repeated Lucy, returning the look.

Her voice was very soft.

An immense relief flooded through Mrs Blacker's whole body.

"She won't tell him. She believes it still and it will always be between us, and she'll put it between me and the children too, when they come. But never mind, she's conquered her anger and made up her mind not to tell, for Ronnie's sake. It won't spoil things for Ronnie."

The two women were sitting over their cups of tea and trying to reduce their agitation to more normal level when hasty steps sounded outside the house and Ronnie rushed into the room. He was flushed and laughing.

"Ronnie!" they both exclaimed.

"I've got it!"

"No!"

"Yes, yes indeed! It was my references, I expect—I don't know—the questions that selection committee asked—I thought they'd go on for ever. I saw the school in the morning—it's splendid, splendid! Quite new! Everything you could wish for the children! I've got it, I've got it!" cried Ronnie.

Seizing his wife in his arms, he danced her round the room, pulled his mother up from her chair and swung her round too.

"Your first application, Ronnie?" cried Lucy, admiring.

"Yes! What do you think of that? When I first got there my confidence was pretty low, I can tell you. There was a man—"

"Sit down and tell it all from the beginning, Ronnie," urged Lucy.

"Yes, do, love—I'll get you something hot to eat," said Mrs Blacker rising.

Popping back and forth between table and stove, Mrs Blacker heard scraps of narrative of the most encouraging description.

"It was no use trying to please them—I just said what I thought—new buildings—more than eight hundred kids—mixed, of course—very good drama work—lots of posts going in the town for you to choose from, Lucy."

Mrs Blacker brought him sausages all a-sizzle, and he calmed a little and ate ravenously.

"Well, how have things been with you two today, girls?" he said at length.

This was like Ronnie; he was never one to focus all interest on himself.

There was a pause.

"Oh, just as usual," said Lucy quietly.

"As usual," repeated Mrs Blacker.

"Good."

"Have some more sausages, Ronnie," urged his mother, rising and stretching out her hand for his plate. "There's plenty in the house, I bought two pounds this afternoon."

"Well! I think I will," said Ronnie, laughing and passing his empty plate. "Oh, by the way—that reminds me." He reached into his pocket. "Here's the pound note I took out of your drawer this morning, Lucy. I thought I might need it for taxi transport, but I didn't. The school was quite near the station, so I walked. No time to tell you, this morning. I only just caught the train."

"Thanks," said Lucy in a casual tone.

She took the note and placed it in safety beneath her saucer. Then looking up at Mrs Blacker with a strange glowing expression of mingled love and remorse, she took her mother-in-law's outstretched hand between her own, and gently kissed its wedding ring.

"You're a good girl, Lucy," said Mrs Blacker.

"You're both good girls," said Ronnie happily.

In point of fact, they were all good people.